SEAL YOU IN MY DREAMS

A Magnolias and Moonshine Novella

SHARON HAMILTON

SHARON HAMILTON'S BOOK LIST

SEAL BROTHERHOOD
SEAL Encounter (Book .5)
Accidental SEAL (Book 1)
SEAL Endeavor (Book 1.5)
Fallen SEAL Legacy (Book 2)
SEAL Under Covers (Book 3)
SEAL The Deal (Book 4)
Cruisin' For A SEAL (Book 5)
SEAL My Destiny (Book 6)
SEAL Of My Heart (Book 7)

BAD BOYS OF SEAL TEAM 3
SEAL's Promise (Book 1)
SEAL My Home (Book 2)
SEAL's Code (Book 3)

BAND OF BACHELORS
Lucas (Book 1)
Alex (Book 2)
Jake (Book 3)

TRUE BLUE SEALS
True Navy Blue (prequel to Zak)
Zak

NASHVILLE SEAL
Nashville SEAL (Book 1)
Jameson (Book 2)

FREDO
Fredo's Secret (novella) Book 1
Fredo's Dream (Book 2)

AUTHOR'S NOTE

I always dedicate my SEAL Brotherhood books to the brave men and women who defend our shores and keep us safe. Without their sacrifice, and that of their families—because a warrior's fight always includes his or her family—I wouldn't have the freedom and opportunity to make a living writing these stories. They sometimes pay the ultimate price so we can debate, argue, go have coffee with friends, raise our children and see them have children of their own.

One of my favorite tributes to warriors resides on many memorials, including one I saw honoring the fallen of WWII on an island in the Pacific:

> "When you go home
> Tell them of us, and say
> For your tomorrow,
> We gave our today."

These are my stories created out of my own imagination. Anything that is inaccurately portrayed is either my mistake, or done intentionally to disguise something I might have overheard over a beer or in the corner of one of the hangouts along the Coronado Strand.

I support two main charities: Navy SEAL/UDT Museum in Ft. Pierce, Florida. Please learn about this wonderful museum, all run by active and former SEALs and their friends and families, and who rely on public support, not that of the U.S. Government. www.navysealmuseum.org

I also support Wounded Warriors, who tirelessly bring together the warrior as well as the family members who are just learning to deal with their soldier's condition and have nowhere to turn. It is a long path to becoming well, but I've seen first-hand what this organization does for its warriors and the families who love them. Please give what your heart tells you is right. If you cannot give, volunteer at one of the many service centers all over the United States. Get involved. Do something meaningful for someone who gave so much of themselves, to families who have paid the price for your freedom. You'll find a family there unlike any other on the planet. www.woundedwarriorproject.org

CHAPTER 1

PETER WATSON WATCHED a human mermaid cavorting with the big fish in the Atlanta Aquarium. Her long blonde hair was pulled back in a ponytail and spread through the water like a giant yellow sea fern. Her shapely body was poured into a bright blue and yellow diving suit with the Aquarium logo on the right thigh. Her graceful movements took his breath away. She fed large angelfish and smaller shy bottom scrapers, making sure everyone got their fair share. Several sharks lurked in the background, used to the fact that they would not be hand fed anything.

He was transfixed. A class of grade-schoolers encircled him. He heard several of the children remark, "cool," or "I wanna do that some day."

As a Navy SEAL, Peter was familiar with wetsuits and diving equipment. He was used to seeing his buddies on SEAL Team 3 swimming like a pod of dolphin with their rebreathers, going undetected from the surface. He knew how to plant an underwater demolition charge, fire his H&K underwater with deadly accuracy, and use a submersible one-man sub. He'd done HALO jumps into shallow water and boarded ships operated by pirates and other assorted bad guys. But never had he played with a mermaid in a neon blue and yellow wet suit.

He felt like some hidden force placed a big hook in his heart and tried to yank it out of his chest. He noticed, as the children moved off to the next large window, that he'd been holding his breath.

Tyler and T.J. came up behind him, but he didn't notice. When T.J. barked, Peter jumped nearly an inch off the ground.

"Elementary, dear Watson. That," he said as he pointed to the girl, "is a thing of beauty."

Peter had to agree, once he settled down. All three of them stood in a line, about two feet from the Plexiglas window, drooling in sync.

She emptied the contents of her fanny pack, zipped it up, and waved to her gentlemen audience. The three waved back.

"Peter," started Tyler Gray, another SEAL from Team 3, "we got one night in Atlanta, and then it's back to San Diego. But if anyone can do it, you can."

"Do what?"

"Catch a mermaid," he whispered.

It was exactly what Peter was thinking.

T.J. motioned to a set of metal steps. Tyler and Peter followed behind him until the stairway veered off to the right, giving the audience a view of the tank from the top. At the left was a door marked private. T.J. glanced both right and left before opening the door quickly and holding it for his buddies.

"Wow, you know this place?"

T.J. stopped, causing Peter to run into him. When the big SEAL turned, his glib expression told Peter he was about to get a whole lot of attitude.

"Dude, I do know how to chase a filly. Now that I'm a married man, I live vicariously through you single guys."

"Like I need help with that?" challenged Peter.

"I'm positive you need help with that. But let's just say I'm selfish. Old married Tyler and I will help you get introduced, and then we bow out. Up to you to get back to the hotel by at least oh-nine-hundred. And you can't be wearing these."

T.J. referred to Peter's bright yellow aloha shirt, his green cargo pants, and the red flip-flops. And his orange toes, which one of the SEAL daughters had painted for him before they left.

His teammate didn't wait for an answer, faced the hallway in front of them, and took off in a brisk walk. A series of office cubicles with glass doors lined the hallway, until they hit the double doors, which automatically opened to the outside. There in front of them, the mermaid was rinsing off, and removing her flippers, her weight belt and fanny pack and had pulled off her facemask. Her hair was now free and glowing golden under the shower.

She placed a big fluffy white towel to her face and then popped her head up to examine them.

"Hello, fellas. What about the word private didn't you understand?"

"Ma'am," T.J. began, "we just came to see if you were okay. We experienced a minor earthquake down below watching you feed the fish."

Tyler couldn't restrain his snicker. Peter was still dumbstruck. The girl was muscled, with tanned skin and bright blue eyes. Her whole face lit up when she smiled. Peter wondered why she wasn't more afraid of three strange men watching her rinse off.

She laid eyes on each one of them and came back to Peter. "You let your SEAL buddies get you into trouble, or are you a frog, too?"

"Now how the hell would you know that?"

She reached out and pinched T.J.'s bone frog logo on his polo shirt, snagging his nipple at the same time.

"Ow!"

Without reacting to T.J.'s outburst, she removed Tyler's hat with the same logo, showing it to him. And then she pointed to the frog print tats on each of their forearms.

Peter extended his right forearm to show her he had identical ink. All the guys on Kyle's squad had those tats, all done by the same artist in Coronado.

"Well then, that explains it." She threw her towel around her neck and picked up her things. "Show's over, gents. I do the rest of it in private, and I have a job to go to in one hour, so adios." She gave a mock salute and just walked away.

"Shit, Peter. You're gonna be single at fifty if you don't get yourself organized," said T.J.

"You know, I'm a big boy, asshole. You don't need to lecture me." Irritation mounted. He was disturbed by the fact the lady didn't introduce herself—or ask them questions, like everyone else did when they discovered they were SEALs.

"I'm sure she'll like that a lot, but first, my man, you gotta get her nekked."

"I'm not—"

T.J. looked like he was going to punch him. "Yes, you are. You're thinking with your little head, and that's okay. We want you normal, not a priest."

"Oh, that's cold, man. You Catholic, Peter?"

"Hell no. And, no, I just want to get to know her."

"Hard to do that when you didn't even hardly say a word or try to stop her," added Tyler. "Just sayin'."

"Getting to know them is overrated," spat T.J. "We're here for one night. You barely have time for that drink I promised you. Don't forget it was your idea to go to the Aquarium instead of hanging out at Dante's."

Their conversation was causing attention and an older gentleman in a white lab coat with horn-rimmed glasses was making his way over to them.

"We were on our way out, sir. Thought we knew the lady," said Peter.

"Who? Abbey?" He turned and scanned the hallway behind him. "I didn't think she was still here."

T.J. walked briskly toward the doorway they'd come through.

"Have a nice day," said Tyler.

The man in the lab coat watched them leave without saying a word.

"Abbey. That's her name," whispered Peter as they descended the stairs. "I'm going to try something."

He approached the visitor information desk. A young girl stood behind the round command center desk and blinked nervously at him, quickly checking out T.J. and Tyler, who stood directly behind.

"Can I help you?"

"I'm Peter Watson, and we were just talking to Abbey upstairs."

"Oh yes. Abbey Hart."

"Right. She had to run off to work. We're underwater stuntmen working for a movie crew in town, and Abbey was giving us some pointers. We think our director might like to meet her." Peter paused, hoping his ruse would work. He tilted his head and gave her a crooked smile. The girl blushed. He lowered his voice to a whisper. "We've only got two more days of shooting, and I think Abbey could be in another James Bond film. Don't you think?"

"Totally! Oh, that would be so cool!" the girl gushed.

He was heartened. "You know where we might find her since she's gone off to work? My co-workers and I think she'd be perfect for the part. Truth is the actress we have slated will need a body double. Poor thing can't swim."

"Who?"

"Who, what?"

"She's wondering who the actress is," T.J. spoke up. "It's Brooke Decker."

Peter glared at T.J. He didn't have a clue who she was, and neither did the girl behind the counter.

"Playboy Miss October last year," added T.J.

"Oh. I see. Sorry, I just thought it might be some-one famous."

"Tom Hiddleston is Bond."

"Oh, Abbey would be thrilled! She's always talked

about being a Bond Girl." The clerk quieted and then waited for another staff member to walk behind her. She whispered and leaned forward, addressing Peter. "I know she works at that place that is owned by the SEAL guy. What's his name?"

All three of the SEALs answered in unison.

"Dante."

BY PURE LUCK, Dante's was a well-known, local watering hole and big time SEAL hangout that grew into an Atlanta tourist attraction as the little bar expanded. Dante himself was one of the early Vietnam SEALs, who helped spawn the legend of the frogmen in those early days. He retired and did what a lot of the early SEALs did, opened up a bar. As his notoriety grew, Dante's transformed with the addition of a pirate ship, barbershop, ice cream parlor, and jazz club.

The SEALs had it on their agenda to give the old man a hearty ahoy. Although legendary in the community, he was also known for not talking about his service years. Now that they'd learned Abbey worked there, Peter had even more reason to show up.

A small jazz combo played on the stage to the side. A few couples were dancing. Tables littered the catwalks crisscrossing the hull and built around the ship. The whole environment felt like a pirate's lair on a lost island somewhere. Girls in pirate garb waited on tables and mounted steps with trays above their heads, carrying brews and food. It would be impossible to hear much in the way of conversation, and being a Friday night, the place was packed.

At first, they were told it would be an hour before they could be seated, but they were offered the long bar, called "The Plank," to forage for a seat or perhaps a table. They got lucky finding a table right away.

Peter was on the lookout for Abbey, scouring the room for her long blonde ponytail. They ordered beers and sat back to soak in the culture. Pictures of old SEAL Teams were plastered over the bar and even encroached across the mirror. Patches from various teams also were affixed, tee shirts signed, along with pictures of Dante with famous, as well as infamous, SEALs. The Polaroid picture of Saddam Hussein in his prisoner garb was copied and had a prominent place on the mirror, along with assorted other bad guys either caught or killed, their gruesome photos some-how not looking out of place. It was a watering hole worthy of any SEAL member, or family of one. All four bartenders were busy, big arms covered in tats and sporting mostly shaved heads or close-cropped hair-styles. No colored hair or fancy buzz cuts. The tats and ear piercings told all the crazy stuff. And, of course, the girls were tens or elevens. They came in all sizes and colors, but to a lady were gorgeous party girls of the highest caliber.

Dante knew merchandising all right, Peter thought. There would never be anything like this place anywhere else in the world.

T.J. recognized Dante from his pictures and invited him over to their table. The man's white hair and full moustache made him hard to miss. With his dark wraparound glasses, he looked more like an aging jazz or rock musician.

"You boys know your money is no good in here, right?" the infamous pirate boomed. Several tables nearby picked up on the conversation.

T.J. pretended not to hear him and shouted back, "Sorry, could you speak a little louder?"

Grins sprouted around the table.

Peter leaned to Dante's ear. "We met one of your girls, Abbey, at the Aquarium today. Is she working tonight?"

Dante nodded and scanned the room. "Not one of *my* girls, although back in the day, she would have been just the type."

The table chuckled in unison.

"You must be like a kid in a candy store, Dante," said Tyler.

Dante scowled and clutched his heart. "The old ticker can't handle too much of that, son. Besides, got a woman for over fifty years who satisfies me just fine. I like to look, but the bottom line is I'd rather come home to a hot meal and a warm bed than an empty house and a bottle. Get my drift?"

Peter nodded. True to the Brotherhood in general was the fact that fidelity, especially long-term fidelity, was prized in the community. Of course, not everyone could walk that line. Divorces were common, but a good woman was a prized possession and something to be cherished and protected. Peter liked that about Dante.

"I saw her arrive earlier. Pretty girl. You know her?" he asked Peter.

"Hoping to."

"She's friendly, but I think she's a good girl. She gets lots of attention, but always goes home alone, if you know what I mean."

"No boyfriend?" he asked.

"I never speak for a woman when it comes to the heart. And I never kiss and tell, either, though at my age, I have to be careful with the blood pressure."

"Understand you might be going on your second retirement," asked T.J.

"Sadly, yes, we're closing at the end of the summer. I'm going to miss it. But other ventures are calling me." He sipped on his mineral water. "Where do you guys head out to next?"

"We think Mexico, Baja," said Peter.

"Baja? Sure beats those long flights to Nam or South America when I was in. We always vacationed in Baja. Fishing."

"We go fishing, too, for bad guys," T.J. chuckled.

Dante's attention was piqued. "There's Abbey. Want me to get her to come over?"

"Appreciate the hand-up, sir," said Peter.

"Well, best of luck. I remember those days. I was blessed with a great memory, and I think I remember every kiss stolen at moonlight on the beach and every pretty girl I romanced. Every one." He placed his palms together and looked up to the ceiling in thanks.

Dante said his good-byes and walked unsteadily, holding on to the handrails all the way up to the top flight of his pirate ship. Peter watched him point in their direction, and Abbey nodded, giving him a kiss on his cheek. Dante waved in return at the SEALs then gave a thumbs-up when Abbey's back was turned.

She traveled the catwalks, switching back and forth, her hips swaying in a short print skirt like all the waitresses with a white blouse pulled down in gathers over her shoulders. Her hair was down, and the silky strands fell nearly to her waist.

She placed her tray on their table. "So this isn't really about a James Bond film, is it?"

Peter answered, "So your friend lied to us about having a way to contact you."

She looked at him like she was sucking on a lemon.

"Okay, we're here merely for the company," he admitted.

"Well, I spent this afternoon feeding fish. I guess I could stand to feed a few frogs. You want some calamari or were you after a heavier fare?"

"I think Peter here will eat just about anything you serve up, Abbey. And, by the way, I'm T.J. This is Tyler. We're both married. But this one?" He pointed to Peter. "No woman has chosen him yet, so he's single."

"Well, imagine that," she said, her smile broadening. "Thanks for the warning." She winked at Peter.

Abbey returned with a huge platter of fried calamari, along with roasted mild peppers and herbed sweet potato fries. "This is Dante's welcome platter. We think he gives away more calamari than he sells, but that's his business."

"You're gonna be out of a job soon, we hear," said Peter, reaching for a bright orange sweet potato wedge.

"I'm outta here soon anyway. Headed back to California. This is a summer job."

She heard a whistle, and her head perked up.

"Gotta go. I'll come check on you later."

"I like the way you say that," whispered Peter. He wasn't sure she heard him through the din until she answered.

"So how long is my watch?"

"All night, darlin'. We leave in the early morning." Peter stared into her blue eyes and felt the oceans move inside him.

T.J. and Tyler were slapping each other, but Peter was fixated on Abbey. He decided she had some special powers. She had to be a mermaid after all.

"I've never had a one night stand before." She winked at him.

"You lie," countered Peter.

"Seriously."

"Nothing more to say, other than I promise to make it memorable." He meant every word, pouring on all the charm he possessed. It was that important to him.

She shivered. "I'm bringing you oysters next." Her lithe body sashayed around their table and disappeared into the crowded room.

Peter felt like his heart had just dropped from his chest and was trying to flip flop down the plank of the walkway after her without getting stepped on or getting knocked off into the drink.

CHAPTER 2

ABBEY HART KNEW she'd be spending some long sweaty minutes with the handsome SEAL as she walked away from him. The hair on the back of her neck suddenly stood to attention. The tenderness of her flesh underneath was created by the extra blood flow her libido was pumping out. She needed a hot and sexy night to wash away the trauma she'd experienced over the past couple of months.

The move to California had been all planned. She was not only following Brian to his new job working in the family winery business, but she was also returning to Sonoma County where her mother and father lived. Until she found out that her fiancé had a different idea of marriage and long-term commitment. She'd never pegged him for a player. But he was, big time. And he was indiscrete about it, which made it even more painful for her. Everyone knew about his "side pussy," which was what the boys in his group called it. Even the girls understood that a guy *that* good looking had more options so of course he couldn't be faithful.

But his looks weren't what attracted her to him. It was the confidence with which he did everything, the mastery he had with people, his precision in putting projects together. He was much loved, a born salesman. And he'd ensnared her in his hooks.

She checked out the room at Dante's. The noisy background was something that settled her mind. All she focused on was taking orders and serving customers. She'd made friends with a couple of the other ladies, but every day she realized this was the perfect job for this stage of her life.

She didn't have to think about anything.

No, she didn't want any hooks or chains. Maybe some ribbon or silk ties, but nothing with any strings or long-term commitments. She was moving on with her life. She'd not been dating since their breakup. Especially after his drunken night of regret when he tried to charm her back to his bed and nearly raped her. Her self-defense course had worked, and that little bottle of pepper spray did the rest. She doubted she'd ever have to confront him again, and that was just fine.

She'd watched her mother wither and grow old as her father continued to run around on her—becoming a very poor liar up to when he stopped trying to hide it. On her suggestion, and after the breakup of her own engagement, Abbey had convinced her mom to file for divorce and agreed to move in with her.

That gave her an extra rock wall. No way she'd bring anybody home to the cottage in Healdsburg her mother lived in. And she'd planned to give her mother what she so deserved—someone to love and take care of her. It was an all-consuming job, leaving little time for anything else but work and school. Her mom had been battling her father's infidelities and cancer at the same time. She might have triumphed over one, but not both. Her mom fought, and eventually lost, her battle with cancer only a few months later.

Life isn't fair.

No one had grieved when her engagement was called off and she moved in with her mom. But moving on was harder than she thought it would be. So she decided she'd put her own life on hold, concentrate on her mom, and just start over later when she had time. After her mom passed, Abbey was suddenly free again. She finished her degree, got a great job at a small winery in Healdsburg, and took the summer job in Atlanta to escape the small town prying eyes of Sonoma County—where everyone knew everyone's business.

Tonight would be the first of many un-complicated hookups, she hoped. Maybe this SEAL could free her soul, and for that, well, she knew how to fuck a man's brains out. It might be the most honest exchange she could manage right now. That and a promise to go away afterwards.

Both of us will get what we want tonight.

She dove into the crowd, letting the noise and crush of bodies make her invisible, but she felt his eyes on her all the way until it was done.

ABBEY SWITCHED SHIFTS with another waitress, so she was free at midnight to meet him in the parking lot.

The witching hour.

Peter asked if she could drive since he'd had a few and his friends were going to dump him without wheels. That meant he'd be entirely dependent on her, which normally she didn't care for, but was perfect this night.

"So that means, if we don't get along, I have to drive you back to your motel room."

"If you're that concerned, we could get another room there."

"At the Roxy? No, thanks."

"What's wrong with the Roxy?"

"I'm guessing you got it on one of those online sites, right?"

Peter nodded as they headed for her cherry red Volkswagen. She clicked unlock on her key fob and climbed into the driver's seat, waiting for him to get situated in the passenger seat before she continued.

"Haven't you seen an abundance of well made-up, tall working girls there?"

Peter blinked a few times and revealed a faint smile. "I wondered about that. Wasn't my choice. The price was right."

The long look he gave her was the non-verbal come-on she needed. He focused on her lips as the space between their bodies grew smaller and smaller, and then they touched.

He smelled like cigars and Tequila, tasted a little salty, but, man, his humming passion synced perfectly with her own internal motor. She inhaled, careful not to show that hitch in her breath, and deepened the kiss, following his lead. With her heart pounding and the neglected space between her legs shouting for attention, she was headed into a full-blown swoon worthy of any big screen romance. The earth moved.

As they separated, he gave her an appraising gaze. "Now that's what I call a good and proper hello."

Her insides chuckled at the meaning of the word proper, and it must have shown, because he answered her internal thoughts with a lop-sided smile of his own. The dark blue of his eyes turned midnight black as he licked his lips and watched her crave him. It was so sexy to have a man watch her bloom and let all that female energy come busting out.

"I'm wondering how I ever managed to think about kissing before now, Abbey. You are world-class."

"And you probably know best, right?"

"I like to think my experience makes me more fun, honey," he admitted as he slipped her hair behind her ear. She was going to let him play with her as much as he wanted to. She thought of it as practiced meditation. Giving herself up to the moment without any of the what-ifs or what's nexts. She'd already decided that was the part about being unentangled.

Oddly, he reached for her hand and gently kissed her palm, all the while studying her reaction. "I like to go slow sometimes."

That was fine with her. But, man, her bud began pulsing, driving an electric current all the way up her spine. She almost ripped off her shirt right here in the parking lot. Instead, she let the fantasy warm her.

"Slow is good. Sometimes." Her voice came out in a croak. She extended her fingers to reach his cheek. Then she ran her forefinger over her lips. "I like being kissed slow sometimes." She felt him jolt inside, sending off a tiny vibration and knew he was exercising control. She decided to pour it on further.

"We have a few hours. We could do this here, or we could go to my place. There, I think you definitely would find the price right." She leaned over to her right and planted a neat kiss to his lips and then turned back to the steering wheel.

Peter made a great show of inhaling and then buckling in.

"I think I'd follow you just about anywhere." He didn't look at her, and she noticed he was adjusting his belt and some other things, as well.

He watched her nearly the whole ride over. Several times she peeked over at him, and he raised his eyebrows. "What?" she asked on one occasion.

"You're nice to look at."

"Well, thank the Lord." She was inwardly pleased, but tried not to show it. "I take it you're from the South?"

"Whatever gave me away, darlin'?" he replied in an exaggerated drawl.

"I'm a California girl, so I can't make out your accent. I need a little help."

"I can do that," he whispered as he traced a line from her ear, down her neck, and over her bare shoulder to where the white cotton gather hugged her arms just below. Then he slipped a finger under the elastic and stopped. "Am I warm?" he asked, teasing.

"Not sure about that, but you're definitely on the right track. Do you mean will I take my clothes off in front of you?" She looked back at him as he withdrew his fingers. "Not if you don't tell me where you're from."

"Very well. I'm from Tennessee."

"Ah, the man from Tennessee."

"That's me."

"Are you a singer?"

"Hardly. I can't carry a tune. But I do like music, and I love to dance. I just save my performance skills for other pursuits."

She wanted to know more about him, but all of a sudden became too shy to ask, before pushing it aside. "Are you east coast or west coast?"

"West. I'm on SEAL Team 3 out of Coronado. Had never been to California before BUD/S."

"Ah. My Golden State."

"I knew you came from Cali before you told me."

"Who talked?"

"You did, darlin'. I could tell from your inflection. You've got that California accent that's unmistakable."

She'd heard it before, but never believed it. Her whole world sounded just like she did.

At her apartment complex, she wound around the night landscaping lights, coming to her building of four units, and climbed the wooden steps, feeling the heat of his body behind her. After inserting her key, she turned to face him.

She wanted to remember the excitement of his face so close to hers, the look in his eyes before they'd done anything but kiss and tease. For some reason, it was important, like a marker in time along a roadside with a whole lot of unmentionable ones to come. His would be the face at the doorway of the new Abbey. The carefree Abbey, the unwounded Abbey. And she'd use his attraction to her to heal the fissures and roughness in her soul, to make-believe that life was perfect and someone could love her absolutely without regard for tomorrow, even just one night.

He showed an honest face, but she still felt the skepticism niggling at the back of her brain. Her track record sucked when it came to her choice in men. But there would be time to think about that tomorrow. Tonight, if she could allow herself to trust, she'd know that she was still human. She'd get reacquainted with the old Abbey who could fall in love, throw caution to the wind, and forget how much it hurt to believe in those who let her down.

It was, after all, what she needed to do. Move on.

He frowned. "You okay? Something wrong?" He didn't touch her or place her hair behind her ear like she knew he wanted to.

"I'm coming to this, collecting myself from a bad experience." She was surprised the words escaped before she could stop them.

Damn!

He stood straighter and glanced around. "And are we going to be interrupted?"

She giggled, looking down at her feet.

He tipped her chin and lifted her face to his. "I'm serious. I don't want to tread where I shouldn't. You married? I don't poach on another man's kingdom."

She allowed the strength in his fingers to steady her, forcing her to examine his dark eyes. "What I meant was that I was engaged. *He* threw it all away, not me. I got out with my dignity, and not much else."

The faint nod he gave her and the twinkle in his eye made her knees buckle slightly. If he hadn't slipped an arm around her waist and pulled her tight against him, she'd have collapsed. He kissed her, whispering back, "Then let's get that thought out of your head, sweetheart. Because, whoever he is, he's one dumb sonofabitch. I'm here to prove him wrong."

God, she needed to hear that! She needed the taste of his tongue in her mouth, the way his lips pressed against her teeth, and to hear his hoarse breathing and the hitch and groan of a man in need as her hands traveled to the front of his jeans. He kissed her neck then across her shoulder and pulled down her blouse, exploring closer to the top of her bra. If anyone could do this, he could.

She slipped from his grasp, turned, and fumbled the door open. He shut it behind him and began the slow, relentless walk toward her that would change her life forever.

"Swear to God, Abbey, I wanted to go slow, but now I'm not so sure. Forgive me if—"

She stepped to him, slamming against his chest, kissing his neck, unbuttoning his shirt, and then pulling up the tee shirt underneath. Her fingers were headed for the buttons on his jeans.

"Doesn't work that way, darlin'. I don't get nekked before you do. That's not the way I do things."

"So let's do something different then."

"No, we're gonna do it my way."

She kept unbuttoning his fly, yanking on his shirt and tee shirt. His chest was bare, revealing in the moonlight a well-muscled torso, huge shoulders, and a six-pack as well-defined as any underwear model. He swatted away her hands as he removed her blouse and tried to spin her around to get at the back of her bra. She grabbed his hips at her sides and slid his jeans off, taking his boxers with them. But he still had on his cowboy boots, which presented a problem when he tried to step toward her to yank on her skirt.

He nearly fell against her. But he was the first one naked. She slipped out of her skirt and removed her bra herself. With his pants around his ankles, they fell onto the bed. Abbey was on her belly with Peter smoothing over her rear, probing for her opening. He bit her shoulder, then grabbed her hips and pulled her to him.

She extended her tailbone into his groin and parted her thighs. In seconds, he was inside, pulling her up from the bed, gripping her hips, and holding her tight against him.

She felt the same desperation he acted out, the need for him to be as deep as possible, to plunder and plow through her soft tissues that had been neglected for so long. His short breaths and deep thrusts sent her bud pulsing. She removed his hand clutching her right breast and placed it between her legs, holding two of his fingers against her nub and pressed.

It all came rolling back, the need to be devoured, the need to drive the other crazy, the need to take and give, to fear her heart would burst with that blissful feeling that nothing in the world mattered except how deep his cock was seated inside her.

CHAPTER 3

PETER WOKE UP before sunrise when the blush of a new day was upon them. Abbey had curled up under his arm, her hands tucked beneath her chin, her thighs like a vice hugging his knee, which pressed against the damp softness between her legs. She slept silently, and for a time, he thought perhaps she was awake, she was so quiet.

Her skin brightened as the morning sunlight illuminated everything, turning her hair into strands of pure gold. He could watch her forever.

They'd been sent to Atlanta for some training on pain with amputees. T.J. had begged for the spot since Coop was staying home, and he recruited Tyler and Peter to be cross-trained, to have a backup specialty, as was the case on all the SEAL teams. T.J. was the official medic on this go-around, but everyone on Kyle's squad had to know how to fill in, in case Coop or T.J. was incapacitated. That was the strength of their team.

Tyler was also a crack shot and worked with Armando, who was their No. 1 sharpshooter.

But today, he didn't want to do anything with his team. He wanted to stay in this bed with this lovely lady he'd pleasured all night long until they both nearly fell asleep in each other's arms, giggled, and called it quits. That was a very nice way to fall asleep. He'd pay for it later.

His phone rang, and he panicked, thinking for a second that perhaps he'd overslept. Had he fallen asleep with his eyes open, just staring down at Abbey? It was T.J.

"Change of plans, Pete. We've got another two days here."

"What happened?"

"They want us to interview some aid workers who work with runaways. Some of them are working with girls smuggled into the US from other countries. Kyle wants us to see if we can get any information on the Garcia cartel from Baja."

Peter had been whispering, but now Abbey was fully awake, kissing his stomach, his belly button as she crawled on top of him and started to rub her sweaty and sweet-smelling self all over his lower body. When she finally did glance up, her eyes were molten.

"Uh, okay then, T.J. Another two days it is." He gave Abbey a wide grin, but his buddy was still on the line. He gasped as she squeezed his balls and stroked his length. Her lips found him, and within seconds, she was riding his thigh while swirling her tongue around his rod and making him forget he was on the phone.

"You still there, Peter? Something wrong?"

That's when he realized T.J. had been filling him in with details he'd have to repeat.

"Um, yea."

She had him all the way to the back of her throat and sucked hard.

T.J. chuckled. "I figured you'd be occupied, but also thought you could use a few more hours of shuteye. Can you get your ass over to the Pancake Hut by our motel? Say by noon? Can you do that, dragon breath?"

"I think I can do that," Peter whispered, barely able to control himself.

"You want a wakeup call in a couple of hours just to make sure?"

He couldn't think. She was working so hard on him, and his cock felt huge lodged deep down her throat. He was mesmerized by the sight of her lips devouring him, her cheeks sunken. Her little moan nearly made him explode.

"Gotta go now, T.J. Talk soon," he said quickly in a helpless whimper, taking careful attention to turn off the phone before dropping it on the carpet beside the bed.

"Holy smokes, honey! Where in the world did you learn to do that?" He sucked in air and then tried to lie back, but he was full into the action.

She kept her focus without smiling, which Peter appreciated.

IN THE SHOWER, Abbey proposed he and his Team-mates show up at the Aquarium after their interviews.

"And do what? Chase you around the tank?" Peter was rubbing shower gel all over her chest then smoothing it down her thighs.

She returned the favor as the shower water rinsed her back. "Come talk to the kids. We have a Jr. Nature Club meeting today, since it's Saturday. The kids get to watch all sorts of films on fish hatching and sometimes cleaning bones and shells brought in by Scientists who are studying the ecosystem. You could tell them what you do, if you're comfortable with that. Since it involves underwater diving, I think they'd enjoy it."

"You want me to talk about cleaning your bones, making you cum a dozen times, that kind of what I do?" he whispered.

She raised her right shoulder like she'd been tickled behind her ear. "No, silly. They're just kids."

"Well, how do you think they got here, missy? And as for cleaning dead fish and picking over bones, well—" He drew her thigh up over his and tickled her sex. "I'm suddenly hungry!"

She stopped him from going to his knees.

"I'm serious, Peter."

He watched her expression and couldn't tell if she was playing with him or not. Part of her looked so innocent, and that other part looked like it was bustin' to get loose.

"Whatever you want, honey. I'm all yours." He stepped back and let a good foot come between them.

"So you think you can escape? Is that what's going on now?" she delivered with a smirk. Her eyes dropped to his dick, which was very interested despite the lack of attention. His blood pulsed quicker as she licked her lips.

"Oh hell, come here!" He grabbed her, slid his fingers up the back of her neck and scalp, and sucked her tongue deep into his own mouth. She tried to pull away, but he wouldn't let her. She finally moaned into him and deepened her connection. When they parted, he felt like there was steam coming from his ears.

"Wow."

She moved back into the water and smiled, inviting him.

"Since I have obviously no choice in the matter, when would this be?"

"About four to four-thirty. You don't have to take up the whole half hour."

She turned around to rinse off her well-soaped chest, and Peter washed her backside, using the opportunity to drop the gel, rinse off, and slide along the fold in her behind.

"I see. So you want me to talk about what we love to do, is that right?"

She nodded.

"Like this?" He plunged deep inside her and heard the satisfying hiss of her inhale across her teeth. "Oh God, Peter."

Once he was fully inside, he pressed her against the tile wall, lifted her right thigh, and rode her from behind, demanding to go deep. He stroked her slick insides, pulling her down on him hard.

With the water still running after several frantic minutes, he felt her melt against him, clutch his thigh, and angle back into him, her head resting backward on his shoulder. She was whimpering.

"Morning, sweetheart," he whispered. "I've sort of got a one track mind. I can't seem to get enough."

She groaned the deeper he got, balancing her body by pushing against the wall as he thrust several more times until he felt the familiar spasms tearing through her lower body. He picked up the pace, causing her explosion. She stilled at their point of climax, holding fast until she could no longer do so. Letting go, they writhed together. Peter kissed and bit the back of her neck and shoulders as their entwined orgasm became one.

Their breathing slowly returned to normal. He kissed the sides of her neck, down along one shoulder, the top of her spine, and down several vertebrae. He rubbed her thighs in long strokes before slipping one hand between her legs from the front to pinch her bud, causing her to jump. She limply leaned back on him, draped her arms over his, and groaned as they separated.

He turned her. With the shower spraying to her right, she did look like a mermaid. Her blue eyes called to him under the ribbons of water making her tanned skin glisten. He sucked her lips and feasted on the flesh under her chin.

His one-night stand had suddenly become very, very complicated. And he liked it that way. He drew her face to his chest, wrapping his arms around her warm body, and held her tight under the water.

"Thank you, Abbey."

She was all smiles when he released her. "So will you come speak to the kids?"

"How can I say no? Let me check with T.J., and if we have time, I'll make sure we're there."

"Perfect."

SHE DROVE THROUGH an espresso stand, bought them

both a latte, and headed for the Pancake Hut.

"This is just what I needed," he said as he held up his coffee cup. She had placed hers in the cup holder between them.

"Good. They make the best coffee here."

"So when do you have to be at work?"

"Two."

"Wanna join us at the Hut?"

"I have pancakes and I'll not be able to fit into my wet suit. I try to go light before I have to dive in there and feed the fish. You know they can smell food on you, right? Confuses them."

He rubbed her exposed thigh with his left hand. "I do understand how they could get confused. Happens to me, too."

She was light-hearted this morning. He hadn't asked her anything about who she was or what she was doing with her life. He'd figured he'd have time for that later, but they spent every minute of it making love. It was totally the opposite of what he'd told T.J. and Tyler he was going to do.

"So you work at Dante's tonight?"

"Nope. I get off at five-ish. How about you guys come over tonight and I'll cook you something good?"

"I'd like that. I'll ask them. Not sure if they have plans."

"Can you stay over?" Her eyes sparkled as she tilted

her head forward as she asked the question.

"I think I could be persuaded." He winked back at her.

She dropped him off at the Hut and sped away as Peter entered the restaurant. It began to hit him how little sleep he'd had. He slid into a booth next to Tyler, facing T.J.

"Holy shit. Should I memorialize that look?" T.J. burst.

"What look?"

"That fucked to submission look all over your face. You can't even stand up straight. You kind of creep along, trying not to fall. Like your dick has turned into that fuckin' DOR bell."

Tyler was laughing at T.J.'s comments. Peter wasn't sure he liked them.

"Ding ding," Tyler chimed.

"You're jealous. That's all. You married guys gotta wait a couple of days. But I know you both, and you're not foolin' me one bit."

"Happy for you, man," answered Tyler.

Peter felt a bit awkward before he realized he was so sleep challenged he could hardly think straight. It was just like in BUD/S on Day 4. He shook his head, then decided to pour the cold water over his scalp, and shook it off, sending water all over both T.J. and Tyler.

"Douchebag." T.J. stood and brushed off the water,

but Tyler was a captive audience and couldn't get out.

Tyler emptied the contents of his water down Peter's back, ice and all. He hated how it felt, but he deserved every ice cube.

"Stop it, children!" T.J. barked as he sat down. "Can't take you kids anywhere."

The waitress arrived and began quickly rubbing down the table with a white towel. "You fellas ready to order or you just gonna mess up my diner?"

"We're having pancakes. Your best. Big fat ones," T.J. said.

"Eggs? Bacon? Sausage? Toast? Cinnamon rolls?"

"Keep going," said Tyler.

"You want me to bring it all?" she asked.

"That's right, darlin'. Gotta do something to make up for you having to work so hard to keep us entertained. We're sincerely sorry about the mess." T.J. turned on the charm.

The woman left, her shoes squeaking. She was sporting a wide smile, though.

Peter decided to get some of his questions answered. "So, T.J. what's so important about these workers? And how many days are we here?"

"Until further notice. We're getting intel for our next trip to Baja. We got three different groups we have to interview. I've only been able to set up one. One of the directors is in Mexico now and won't be home until

Monday. After that? It's up to Kyle."

"He's sure these workers know Santiago Garcia?" Peter knew Garcia's brother had been killed in a raid the SEALs had been involved in before Peter joined Kyle's team.

"That's what we're here to check out."

Peter downed the tall glass of orange juice. He tried to think about the human trafficking angle, which made him sad, but his mind was really on Abbey. He couldn't wait to get distracted again. His biggest problem now was trying to stay awake until then.

"Oh, almost forgot. We have an invitation to dinner at Abbey's tonight."

"Nice," answered Tyler.

"I'm game," said T.J. without a moment's hesitation.

"And we've got a speaking engagement at the Aquarium at four o'clock. Talking to kids about what we do. A little community outreach."

"I'm cool with that," answered T.J.

"She actually wants us to come back there? Wouldn't she rather have a little alone time with you?" asked Tyler.

"Well, it's part of her job. They got a Jr. Scientist club or something there, studying fish and all things underwater. She even took them on a field trip to Dante's, before they opened, of course." Peter could see his two buddies were genuinely interested. "She's at work until after the class."

"I think we could make it by four," added T.J. "One of those guys we visited at the center wrote a children's book on SEALs. He gave me a copy. Maybe the Aquarium could start selling them in their store."

"Yeah, bring it along."

"You sure you want to share precious lady time with us?" asked Tyler again.

Peter was starting to lose his patience. He noticed his lack of control was proportionate to his lack of sleep. "I'm not sharing, asshole. I'm giving her a little time to decide if she wants me for more than just a one-night stand. So you guys better be on your best behavior."

CHAPTER 4

BEFORE ABBEY GOT to the Aquarium she got Peter's text saying they'd be at the talk this afternoon at four. And she was thrilled he said they were looking forward to some home cooking.

She checked the time and decided to make a quick trip to the store before work. She grabbed fresh fruit for a salad, four thick New York steaks, some fresh string beans, and a couple bottles of her favorite red wine. She chose one from a winery owned by some SEALs near the one she'd be working at. The label had a picture of a frog skeleton, and she thought it appropriate for tonight's feast.

She placed her groceries in a zip up cooler bag she carried with her everywhere. When she arrived at work, she placed the bag inside the walk-in cooler the scientists used for preserving tissue samples and storing works in progress.

Although she felt the effects of her lack of sleep, her

happy mood boosted her stamina. The churning in her stomach felt like love. It was always the same way with her. The non-attachment principle she'd held onto came crashing down, and in its place was a bright new day filled with possibility. Being around Peter had been a welcome distraction. Now she knew it would be hard to let him go.

She cleared all that out of her mind as she put on her wetsuit and gear, picking up a baggie of fish parts and chopped squid that the biologists portioned out for this afternoon's feeding show. With no special instructions on watching individual species, she readied herself, applied the fanny pack with the food baggie, and dove into the tank.

Saturday shows were busy, and she was a whole two minutes late, so quite a crowd had developed. She swam over to the large blue-green plexiglass window and waved at some of the smaller children, who waved back. She motioned for others in the crowd to come forward, and slowly, the front two rows of audience filled with little faces pressing to get the best view of the tank contents.

One of the biologists had named the large male whale shark in the tank Crestor after the cholesterol drug. He looked especially hungry today, and she made a note to have him fed earlier than normal and would request an increase in his calorie intake. Her tag wand had a tiny electric shock to it, which she retrieved from her belt when he got close and was persistent. Showing him the yellow tip of the wand was all he needed, and he meandered to the corner to await his turn.

With Crestor out of the way, she began stringing out parts of fish guts, keeping one eye on the grey shark. A couple of Blue Runners made off with a long tendril, pulling at the pieces until both swam away with a nursery school of Blue Tangs following behind. She carefully fed the pairs of Butterflyfish, who daintily ate from her gloved hands. A school of Yellowbanded Sweetlips plucked at pieces of meat that had floated to the rocky bottom, their bright, neon yellow lips smacking up the yummy substance.

With her food half-distributed, she examined her audience and waved again. The back row contained several tall men, and she squinted, trying to determine if perhaps the SEALs had arrived early. Going from face to face, she didn't recognize anyone until she suddenly saw the face of her ex-fiancé, Brian.

She blinked several times, not sure she was seeing him correctly, and when she last focused on the line of adults, he was no longer there.

My imagination is playing tricks on me again.

Though it had been over a year since she'd seen her ex, her mind had been playing tricks on her all summer long. She'd get a funny feeling and turn, not finding anyone standing there, but sure he'd been there nonetheless. She thought she saw glimpses of him peering around a wall or in crowds at the shopping mall, only to look again and see nothing of the sort. Each time her heart began racing. Today was no different.

No way. He doesn't even know where I am.

She'd heard the rumors of his new love interest and had been so grateful when she stepped on the plane in San Francisco, headed for Atlanta and the rest of her life. They had wineries, too, in Georgia. She noted that if she had to abruptly leave California she was certain she could get work there.

She finished the rest of the feeding, double checked a repair that had been made to the coral reef, which seemed to be holding, glanced back at her audience, and took a bow. There was no sign of Brian anywhere.

The warm shower afterward was one of her favorite parts of her day. She shampooed her hair, put on her jeans and her light blue Aquarium logo tee, and took extra care with her makeup. She even added a tiny bit of perfume then headed out to the showroom to give guided tours before the scheduled Jr. Nature Club event. Several groups of children on an exchange program came through with their sponsors. Abbey worked with translators to point out all the fish in the tank and show them pictures of what she did.

She kept searching the crowds for Peter's face, halfway feeling like he'd jump out and surprise her. Her senses were heightened. The closer it got to four o'clock, the louder her stomach growled.

She convinced one of the college interns to help set up chairs in the meeting room just off the main lobby with glow in the dark murals on the curved walls that bordered the big tank. She checked the projector and the film reel she always played, which told the little visitors what kinds of opportunities were available to them during the rest of the summer months. The lights were set low, and soon her young audience started filling up chairs, being directed by the reception area and another intern dressed in a fuzzy shark costume. "Crestor" was always a hit with the little ones. Occasionally, they hired a magician to dress up in the costume and do magic tricks with the young audience.

She began the film clip and adjusted the dimmer again, setting the room darker still before backing into a corner to wait.

"Hey, Abbey, how you been?"

Brian's voice sent an electric bolt down her spine. Whipping around, she saw no one behind her. Due to the structure of the room, his voice had been thrown from across the sea of chairs. She could barely make out his form, leaning against a painted Roman column from an underwater scene, but the way he folded his arms over themselves and crossed his legs would identify him anywhere. His forehead and eyes were bathed in dark shadow, and she had a sudden sense of doom. His unannounced appearance in Atlanta, after she'd been very careful not to tell any of his friends where she had gone, was not a welcome sign. It had been over a year since she'd last seen him.

She stood straight, her hands flailing at her sides, the laughter from the children underscoring that sinking feeling in her gut that he was here for nefarious purposes. He untangled his long limbs, stalked around the last row of chairs, and headed directly toward her, stopping an arm's length away and just staring at her.

"You had no idea how hard it was to find you, Abbey."

Oh yeah, you sonofagun. I did that on purpose.

Now she wished she'd decided to not return to Sonoma County. Her new employer would be the only way he could have gotten the information about her whereabouts.

"You could have tried to track my cell phone," she said as coldly as she could deliver.

He tilted his head, as if deciding which view he liked better, then righted himself and smirked. "I tried that."

Another shard of panic coursed through her body. Being on Brian's radar wasn't healthy for any living thing. She was now more convinced of it than ever. Why she had never seen this dark side of him before, she couldn't figure out. His practiced charm had masked what she now saw as his true nature. She'd held off reporting him to the police because of his veiled threats. Then she'd been consumed with her mother's care. Finally, as she learned of his new love interest, she didn't see the need any longer and just went on with her life, hoping to never run into him again.

But now she saw how lethal he was. His dangerous eyes spewed hatred. How could she have ever loved such a man?

"Well, now you've found me, so you can go right back to the pit you crawled out from."

He tented his eyebrows in a mock sour expression. "Wow! Not even a little bit happy—or maybe 'happy' isn't the word. Flattered?" He leaned back to see how well the words hung on her bones and shook his head. "Whatever! Not one bit curious why I worked so hard to find you?"

"Not really, Brian." She got hold of her stomach and felt her spine develop a firm straightness. "Now is not a good time. I'm working, as you can see." She pointed to the audience of rapt children.

"I'd like to take you to dinner tonight."

"Sorry, she's all tied up." Peter's deep soothing elixir of a voice quickened her heart. She wanted to kiss the ground he walked on, but instead, she allowed him to wrap his huge arms around her body and crush her to his chest, planting a wet sloppy kiss that got the attention of several of her audience.

Thank God you're here, Peter!

She licked the taste of him from her lips and closed her eyes, showing Brian the effect Peter's kiss had on her, and warmly accepted the feel of his fingers running down the cleft in her backside. It was something Brian would not be able to miss as well.

"Brian, this is Peter, my—"

"Boyfriend." Peter inserted before she could say otherwise. He extended his hand, and Abbey could tell the squeeze he delivered to Brian was uncommonly painful. "Nice to meet you, Brian."

Abbey thought Brian would have been discouraged, but to the contrary, the bitter expression on his face peeled away more of the mask and showed her more of his dark side. Or perhaps the darkness was growing.

"Likewise, Pete," Brian said in an obvious insult.

She would have explained something reasonable about Brian's visit if she had more respect for him, but she let him dangle, and he offered no explanation. Peter's fingers tickled her rear again, telling her he'd get it out of her later, most likely when she was naked if she was going to be stubborn about it. She stepped closer to him and rubbed her thigh against his, sending her left breast right into his bicep.

"Peter and his buddies are Navy SEALs, Brian," she said proudly and watched. If there was any impact at all, Brian expertly hid it.

T.J. and Tyler joined their little group. T.J. held a thin book, but all sets of eyes drilled into her ex.

"I'll take a raincheck on that dinner then," Brian said softly, trying to show how little an effect it had on him, and turned to leave.

Peter grabbed his arm before he could leave. "Not in your lifetime, meathead." He jerked his fingers from their grip on Brian's elbow. The grin that was returned was pure evil.

All four of them watched Brian turn the corner and leave the room.

"Who the hell was that?" asked Tyler.

"Someone who thinks he's more important than he is," answered T.J. as he craned his neck to make sure the newcomer was long gone.

"My ex-fiancé."

"Smart girl," said T.J. "He's dumb as a box of rocks, though, to let someone like you get away."

She was going to say something when the film

came to an end.

"We can talk about it over dinner. It's show time now, boys!"

CHAPTER 5

T HE SEALS WERE introduced, as they had insisted, only by their first names. Even a couple of staffers from the Aquarium appeared at the back of the room to hear what they had to say. Abbey moved off to the side, while the three of them began their talk. It had been a stressful afternoon, capped by the insertion of Abbey's ex. Peter was on the lookout for the guy to show his face again.

He listened to T.J. show the *Navy SEALs for Wimpy Kids,* which was a combination coloring book and simplified story of how a wimpy kid could grow up to become a Navy SEAL. The autobiographical story was written by one of the amputees they'd been studying for pain treatment. As T.J. paged through all the pictures of running rubber boats over the rocky cliffs into the surf, lying on the "Midnight Sand," and staring at the moon while getting "Wet and Sandy," it brought forth a lot of fond memories from Peter's own training some three years ago. The audience of rapt faces scooted their chairs in a tight semicircle around the three of them, and before T.J. could finish going through the whole book, they were peppered with questions.

Peter noted the pages containing pictures of long guns and sidearms were especially of interest. Doing exercises and running with fifty pounds of rocks in the desert was not very popular. Peter chuckled to himself. He felt the same way. But he'd gotten through it, and that was all that counted.

Several times, he inserted stories of jumping out of airplanes at midnight and some of the places they'd visited, officially, of course. He winked at Abbey, who appeared distracted and was biting her lip.

Tyler and T.J. talked about spending time in the McKinley burn center in Texas. They all stressed the value of working hard, not for rewards and trophies, but so they could become the best version of themselves they could be. Peter added that there really was no failure in someone deciding the SEAL training wasn't for them, and that for many men, it was just a course to let a man know where his limits were, not necessarily a goal to achieve. Trying was being the hero.

And he'd had that conversation with many men who had washed out. He honestly felt it was true that

SEALs weren't better than anyone else. They were simply the ones who wouldn't quit.

By the time they'd finished a robust forty-five minutes of Q & A, the room was packed with as many adults as children. When a local news crew arrived, T.J. called it a wrap and refused to go on camera. Tyler and Peter backed him up one hundred percent. Some years ago, one of their ranks was targeted by a lone wolf terrorist who killed his teenage daughter in a suicide bomb attack. Real names and faces were always kept private, for obvious reasons. Nothing like finding your picture in the newspaper in a little village in one of the Eastern block countries where they weren't officially training. Worse, it had actually happened.

They received an enthusiastic round of applause and spent a few minutes afterward signing autographs in permanent marker on young scientists' forearms. Abbey kept the media at bay like a mother hen guarding her chicks. She also allowed the store manager to write down the name of the coloring book so young scientists in the future could pick up the paperback workbook in the "Friends of the Aquarium" section of the bookshelf.

It worried Peter every time he glanced over at Abbey, only to find her searching the crowd milling around the entrance to the large classroom. He needed to know what the story was there. He didn't like the little taste of this gentleman that lingered from the minute or so interaction. Men like him were the same the world over. In the face of innocence, they were emboldened to become mean. Peter not only didn't care for the gentleman, he didn't trust him one whit.

"Here you go," she said as she handed T.J. back his book.

"Thanks. I hope they help him out. He's got a lot of expenses we're trying to negotiate for him with the VA. Every little bit helps."

"I'll make sure our manager knows that as well." Abbey gave them a bright smile. "Thank you for today. And so sorry about the news crew."

"No worries," said T.J., batting the idea away with his hand. "Someone must have called them."

"Well, we only get news coverage when something bad happens here. Or when a celebrity comes." She wiggled her eyebrows and winked at Peter. "Not that you guys aren't celebs, of course."

"Of course," winked T.J. in return.

Peter wrapped his arm around her waist. "We're happy to give you guys a little publicity. Hope the crew found something else juicy to cover."

"Oh no. They were on their way out immediately when they found out they couldn't get your butts on their station."

"I didn't especially want my butt on T.V.," said Tyler.

Peter squeezed Abbey as she blushed at Tyler's remark.

"So you ready for some good home cooking? Nothing fancy, of course. I got some nice steaks. Just need a little time to whip up the chocolate cake." Abbey looked up at him, and he had to lean down and give her a lazy I-don't-care-who-sees-it kiss.

T.J. whistled. "You work fast, Watson," he said.

When Abbey came up for air, she was blushing, breathless, and her hair messed up because Peter had indulged in her silky softness. "That's the way I like it," she answered T.J.

T.J. AND TYLER followed behind them as Abbey drove him to her apartment.

"Don't expect anything too grand. I like simple cooking. I'm not a French chef."

Peter had been watching her profile and enjoying her pink cheeks and obvious bashfulness. "I like the simple things you do just fine. Haven't found anything yet I could ever complain about."

"Oh, I'm sure I have my moments."

"I doubt that." He wanted to ask her about the ex, but wondered if it was going to ruin their mood. He knew it was selfish, but a long lingering kiss before he had to share her with his other two buds might satisfy his need or inflame him for the rest of what he hoped would be another magical evening.

But that guy's hard expression really bothered Peter. Those kinds of men didn't go away or slink off into a corner somewhere. They took advantage of surprise. Not able to confront directly, they would take the tactical advantage of getting their prey when they were not paying attention. He knew how to handle that type. Only problem was here, in the good old US of A, he was limited in his quiver of options.

She didn't have a trace of worry on her forehead until he asked her what he had to ask her. He thought about it for a second and then launched his volley.

"So I want to know about this Brian guy. I'm coming from a place of not just caring about you, Abbey. I think he puts you in danger."

The familiar wrinkle he'd seen during their talk suddenly reappeared between her beautiful brows. She rocked her head from side to side and sucked in air, exhaling with her answer.

"I made a mistake, Peter." She gave him a quick glance then continued. "I thought he was a different person. In many ways, he is the exact opposite of what I saw, but for some reason, I admired his mannerisms, how he dealt with people, and how much people seemed to admire him."

"I don't hear anything in that about love, Abbey.

What about him did you see, really see?"

She frowned.

"Don't even go thinking I don't have a right to know. I'm trained to watch out for bad guys. This Brian fellow is a bad guy, Abbey. I'm not going to let you dismiss him so quickly."

"Oh, I dismissed him, all right."

"Not what I was meaning, honey. You can't underestimate a guy like that. I can see it in his eyes. He likes to hurt people. What I want to know is why you didn't see that."

They'd come to a stoplight. She slowly turned to face him. "Maybe I'm not trained to see that in people. Maybe I want to believe the good in people."

"I like that in you. But not when it puts you in harm's way, sweetheart."

He was as serious as he could be. He didn't smile, staring right back into her blue eyes, and kept the softness and tenderness away. It was important to him Abbey see the real danger there. If he was wrong, he'd ask for forgiveness later, but right now, he had to get her to see what he saw.

When her eyes teared up, he resisted the impulse to take her in his arms. That might just turn into something else. He needed to make sure his message was delivered. He couldn't help her with the confusion or the possible low-grade pain he'd caused.

A car behind them honked; the light had changed to green.

Abbey continued out into the intersection without checking traffic and nearly T-boned a late-crossing truck. She slammed on the brakes. Her face turned bright red, and she was shaking.

"Not your fault, Abbey. Let's get to your place. I distracted you, and I'm sorry for that."

She didn't look at him the rest of the way.

Barely two minutes later, they stopped into the parking lot of her complex. He raced around the car to open the door for her and pulled her up and into his arms. She was still shaking and had stiffened, but he held her until he could feel her melt.

"You did great, sweetheart. We'll talk about it later, okay?"

He pulled the hair from her face and held her between his palms.

"Okay?" he repeated.

She nodded and looked down.

He kissed her forehead. "Come on. Let's get something in our stomachs and satisfy these guys so they can leave us alone."

He felt her squeeze his waist back. "Thank you," she whispered.

Tyler and T.J. caught up to them as they were climbing the stairs. "Everything okay?" Tyler asked.

"Just a close call," answered Peter. "She's okay."

Abbey separated herself from Peter's grip, got out her keys, and unlocked her front door. "I'm fine," she said with defiance. "I wasn't paying attention." She gave them a sweet smile.

"Well, Peter does have that effect on women. Hang on, darlin'. Peter's an acquired taste," said Tyler. He got a punch in his arm from Peter, who made sure it was harder than necessary.

He helped Abbey in the kitchen, insisting the guys sit back and have a beer. She tasked him with stoking up the barbeque, which was something he excelled at. The deck outside had a couple lawn chairs, and T.J. and Tyler accompanied him for moral support.

They didn't say anything, but he knew that's why they were sitting down next to the barbeque. They were waiting for his answer to the unasked question. He'd applied the steaks and then grabbed his beer, leaning against the railing.

"Her ex is a piece of work. I'm seriously concerned for her safety, truth be told."

"I hear you," answered T.J. "Just asking a question, though. You sure it's your place?"

Peter knew he had the right to inquire. He wasn't sure what his answer was going to be, as he was formulating it while talking to them.

"One thing I know for sure is there are evil people

out there. Even if I didn't care for her, and, fellas, I'm falling hard here."

"Yup. Got that," said Tyler.

"Some things you just pick up on. She's in danger. I know she is. I can't let that go."

"I understand. But what can you do about it? We only got a couple of days here. Then we have to get back to San Diego. You can't go bringing her with us. I mean, you're not thinking that way, right?"

Peter could see T.J. was right.

"I'm thinking I might be able to discourage him somehow."

"That's not smart, Peter, and you know it," T.J. reminded him.

"You're probably right." He hated to admit it, but doing the smart thing wasn't what he was known for. Except he didn't want to hurt anyone else or to ruin his career. But somehow he had to get this guy out of Abbey's life.

"Does she have anyone here who can help out?"

"No family that I know of. But I really don't know."

Abbey brought out some chips. Both T.J. and Tyler stood up. Peter turned over the steaks without looking at her or showing what they'd been talking about.

"I'm just about done in here. As soon as the steak's done, we eat," she said and closed the sliding glass door behind her.

T.J. put his hand on Peter's shoulder. "Well, at least you got a little time to talk to her about it. Maybe it's not as much of a problem as you think, Peter. I'm hoping that's the case."

Peter peered out at the gardens and pool below. The sky was a deep rose color in sunset. He hoped he made the right decision. His heart was racing, just like before any good mission. He had confidence in what he could accomplish, if he had the right tools. The bigger question was, what was he going to need? And what was the outcome he desired?

He had to figure those two things out first. Then he could plan the course of action.

CHAPTER 6

A BBEY SAID HER good-byes to the two SEALs, standing arm and arm with Peter at the door, as if he lived there too.

"Not to worry, fellas. I'll make sure he's safe and sound in the morning."

"You do that," said T.J. "We got that place over in Peachtree City to visit tomorrow, and they're expecting us by ten. I can pick him up, say, eight or eight-thirty?"

"I don't work until Noon. Want me to fix breakfast?"

"You've done a lot already. Let's get this guy out of your hair, so I'll grab him at eight, and we'll get breakfast on the road. But I'll deliver him in one piece afterward. How's that?"

"I go from the Aquarium straight to Dante's. Deliver him over there, if you don't mind." She loved the little-boy-lost look Peter had on his face, his head whipping between the two of them.

Tyler shrugged. "Well, Peter, I'd say your day is pretty much all planned out. Lucky for you, your two social secretaries are in sync."

When the door closed, Abbey's palms sweated thinking about the "talk" she knew they were going to have when they were alone. Just as she suspected, Peter pulled her to him. Before he could say anything, she clasped her hands at the back of his neck, tiptoed to kiss him, and then pushed herself away.

"Let's get the kitchen cleaned up first. Then I promise we'll have that talk."

"Sounds good to me, honey."

She put on a jazz channel to ease her nerves, poured herself another glass of wine and gave Peter another long neck. The cleanup didn't take more than a few minutes. The dishwasher droned in the background as they took a seat facing her blank TV. She sat at one end of her couch, slipped off her shoes, and placed her feet in Peter's lap.

"You've known me, what, barely two days, and already I'm giving you foot rubs?" He grinned, but quickly pressed his fingers into places on her ankle and sole she hadn't known existed.

Abbey arched back and closed her eyes. It didn't take much imagination to fully comprehend what kind of a backrub he'd be able to give her.

"Oh. My. God. That feels divine, Peter."

"Good." He was focused on her feet unlike anyone in history had ever been. The devotion he showed her limbs was so extremely sexy. She had the urge to remove all her clothes and let him work over her entire body.

"So why don't you begin at the beginning? You said this guy was your ex. How did he show up here, or is this where he's from?" Peter asked.

"No. He's from California. I have no idea what he's doing here. Just showed up. I haven't spoken to him in over a year."

He nodded. "So what did he say?"

"He said it had taken him a long time to find me. Probably because I didn't exactly tell anyone except my future employer where I was going. But when I was finishing up school and we both lived in town, I never heard from him at first, never saw him except in passing, you know."

"Um hum. Where exactly was that?"

"Oh, sometimes they shopped at the same store. He found another girlfriend right away. In fact, I don't think he even saw me. His girlfriend did."

"Okay, where else?"

"I think I saw him in traffic a couple of times. Like I said, I'm sure he never saw me. He was always looking the other way, Peter. He didn't seem to want anything to do with me. At first."

"At first?"

Abbey stiffened, and she yanked her feet from Peter's tender hands, righting herself to sitting position a few feet from him on the couch. "One night, he was drunk. He stopped by the house right after my mother had died. Tried to pretend he was giving condolences, but he nearly—he tried to force himself on me."

Peter came to full attention. She watched as both his hands turned into tight fists. "Did he hurt you?"

"Scared me. I was right beside my purse, and after I kicked him in the groin, I sprayed him with pepper spray. I shoved him outside and called the police."

"Good for you. That ended it?"

"Oh yes. I never saw him after that. Not at all. Not in passing. Nowhere."

"Did you press charges?"

This was the part that was difficult for Abbey. Twisting her toe into the carpet, she answered him softly, "No." She'd been told by the police it was a mistake, but she was so convinced he'd not come anywhere near her she didn't want to cause the family more drama than they'd already experienced, especially with the fiasco with her dad. "Peter, I think he was drunk and I heard later he'd broken up with the girl he was seeing. Probably one of those somber moods he got into and needed some consoling and got angry when I couldn't give it to him."

"You were wise to trust your judgment."

"Well, he didn't get arrested, but there was a police report made. I did do that, but elected not to escalate it further. I told them I would if he ever bothered me again."

"And now he's here."

"Yes, but I think he has some other reason to be here."

"Abbey, that's not healthy." Peter slid over next to her and put his arm around her shoulder. "You don't know that. Don't make excuses for the guy. He dropped in unannounced and caught you off guard. That was intentional."

She squirmed under his arm and threw it off. "Don't be silly, Peter. There has to be an explanation."

"Probably, but maybe not the one you want to hear."

"Well, we didn't exactly give him any chance to do any talking, now did we?"

"Still making excuses for him. Abbey, you are such a smart lady. Think about this objectively. He *already showed* his true colors. If he almost hurt you once, he will do it again. You don't have to give him the benefit of doubt. That's your hang-up, and you've got to realize that. Unless…" Peter looked at his hands, rubbing them together, his elbows balanced on his knees.

"Unless what?"

"Unless you're wanting to let him be part of your life again."

He didn't touch her. She roared upright, not believing what she'd heard. It was outrageous, and it angered her.

"How could you say something like that? No. Never!"

Peter stood up and put his hands in his pockets at first, then crossed his arms and studied her expression. "So what's the hesitation? I don't understand, Abbey. Help me."

She inhaled and stared down at her feet again. What was she feeling? Regret? Did she miss Brian? Her heart shouted a resounding *no* to that question. What was it?

With the pounding in her chest as background noise, the clouds lifted and she saw clearly what had happened the instant she'd recognized Brian. She didn't know if he would believe her, but it was the truth, and the truth Peter deserved to hear.

"Peter, I didn't want to make him angry. I wanted him to go away."

"You are afraid of him, aren't you?"

It was difficult to tell him, but Peter already knew what she was feeling.

"I think so."

He was in front of her in an instant, kneeling, holding their entangled hands on her thighs. "Abbey, trust me. You're right. You're totally right to be afraid of him. You should never ever again be alone with him. Do you believe me, honey?"

She read in his sincere eyes that he cared about her. But then, she'd thought the same thing about Brian at first. "I know you're right, Peter. I wish I wasn't so cowardly."

"No. You're just super trusting. Like I said before, that's a great quality and something I admire in you. You see the good in people, or think you do. But some people, by their actions, cannot be trusted. He knows all the right things to say, but his actions speak volumes. Stay away from him."

"Not like I can stop him," she whispered.

Peter's forehead became more lined, the edges of his mouth drooped, and he squinted. He scrambled to his feet and paced across the room in front of her. When he finally stopped, he put his hands on his hips and stared down at her. "No, but I can. That's what I'm afraid of."

"No. You shouldn't get involved."

"But I already am involved, Abbey. Can't you see that?"

Of course it was what she wanted to hear, but it was also caused him some distress.

"When I go back to San Diego, you'll be all alone here, and that worries me. I'll be too far away to do anything should you need me."

She knew she should feel more afraid, but seeing Peter standing in front of her, totally focused on protecting her and focusing on her safety, thrilled her. She knew he couldn't help but be her protector. It was carved into his DNA. No matter how much she'd try to convince him otherwise, he wouldn't be persuaded.

She rose to her feet slowly and stepped timidly toward his hulking form. His shoulders were broad, his arms solid steel and corded with veins. He even had muscles in his jaw, his neck, and other places that made her blush. This big man had a heart as big as his massive body.

She could try to object, of course. But what good would that do? Abbey knew he would not change his mind. And it wasn't what she wanted anyway.

No, the only thing she wanted to do right now was submit to him. Be everything she could be to him to thank him for caring. And maybe, just maybe it would be enough to hold them loosely together until she could figure out a way to visit him in San Diego. It was something to think about in the days and weeks to come.

Right now, all she wanted was to have him wrap his arms around her and kiss her senseless.

"I'm sorry, Peter. You're right. No one's cared about me and my safety like you have." She slipped her fingers up his chest, traveling over the bumps his nipples made under the cotton shirt up to the thick bands at his neck, one hand tracing to press three fingers against his lips. "I tell myself I can be responsible for everything. But there are some things I cannot do alone. It's scary to need you so much, Peter. I hope—" she admitted as she moved up on tiptoes and lightly kissed his mouth beneath her fingers—"you'll forgive me. It's all new to me."

His arms wrapped around her waist, smashing her lower body against his groin. She rolled her head back and he kissed that sweet spot she loved, just below her ear and under her chin. She felt the vibration in his chest as he moaned at her taste.

"Let's not think about this any longer tonight. We can always talk about it tomorrow, maybe tomorrow night. We have time. Not very much time, but I don't want to waste it talking about my ex. Make love to me, Peter. I need that more than ever."

He picked her up, one arm under her knees, and effortlessly carried her to the bedroom. Gently laying her on the bed, he and removed his shirt, watching her. She began to take off her blouse, but he stopped her.

"No. My job," he reminded as he unbuttoned her and kissed her flesh underneath, pulling up her bra and teasing her knotted nipples with his tongue and his teeth. "This is my job, Abbey, and I take it seriously."

His fingers were thick and slightly clumsy, but the scars on his hands felt delicious against her tender flesh. He adjusted his button fly jeans so they slipped off his slim hips. Next, he unzipped her pants, peeling them off her thighs and depositing them in a pile on the floor. That fully revealed her white lace thong panties, with her bra pushed up over her breasts and the shirt open wide. He pulled her panties down just far enough so he could get access to her waiting sex.

At last they were one again. There would be no talk about all the things they *should* talk about. As he rode her, he loved all the tension and worry from her body. He left her pliable and sweaty. Her heart loved him with a fever that burned every cell in her body.

The only thing left for her to do was to show him how much she needed him, without worrying if she was holding on too tight. That would be a concern and thought for another day. But not tonight.

Tonight was made for love.

CHAPTER 7

PETER AWAKENED BEFORE Abbey did, watching her sleep. The sky began to turn a robin's egg blue, but was stubborn about it. Birds to chirped on the railing of her balcony, twittering in quick staccato conversations. All seemed right with the world, except something black loomed in the background.

He recalled their conversation last night, confirming the fear she finally acknowledged she'd been masking. He knew all about that. He was a master of it himself. All the guys had to mask things they were afraid of. It had nothing to do with looking more competent or manly—it was a requirement that he be able to focus and partition things off, shield some of his emotions from his decision-making. That was the real trick: learning to shield just enough, never too much. Emotions gave him that gut reaction he'd need in a firefight or a dangerous wartime situation. Not having them made him a liability not only to himself, but his

Teammates.

He was lucky that he had the Brotherhood. Those guys would die for him. It was probably hard for the general public to understand. He also felt lucky that he'd been allowed to participate on the Teams. Lucky that at such a young age he'd found something so exciting and compelling to live his life for.

But now there was Abbey, and this was a different kind of fear. He didn't want to go overboard, get all Commando with her life. Heck, maybe she didn't really want that. Maybe she wasn't ready. But it would be hard to step away.

Should he?

He examined not only the beautiful evening they'd had, but also the way he felt giving the talk to the youngsters at the Aquarium, how proud he'd been of his job and his brothers. He looked inside his heart and saw the women and children and old men he'd saved in Afghanistan, Yemen and North Africa. He pictured those he could not save. He knew a big chunk of that portion of the world didn't have the luxury of doing what they wanted to do. They lived in survival mode. Part of his mission was to help bring about a peace for them by ridding their population of the idiots who were enslaving them, the evil people who cannibalized their religion and made everyone's life hell. Even the unwittingly incompetent assistance from his own country and others he'd seen there. It was a jigsaw puzzle with a million pieces thrown in the dusty sand.

But here, he could walk away. Except that wasn't what he was about. He had to do the one thing that would be the most difficult for him; he needed to assess what Abbey wanted. What she *really* wanted. Not what she *thought* she wanted. If he got any indication she was just sleepwalking through the night with his heart, then he'd have to get out quickly, even if his hunch was correct. Maybe set something up with Dante. Dante would know a resource here in Atlanta to give her aid if he couldn't be the one.

She stirred in his arms, twisted her silky body against his, and shocked his libido into full speed ahead, but he was going to hold back. Her hair was all over the place, even partially covering his face, which was so odd for him, because normally he didn't like anything obstructing his view or tickling his cheeks. She smelled like a woman in lust, remnants of her perfume still lingering on the sheets as she moved. Her body was like a furnace, and it got hotter and damper between her legs as she hugged his upper thigh between hers. The delicate lips of her sex pressed against him.

Yes, he was a lucky man. But today he'd have to do the real man-thing—the right thing. He'd never forgive himself if he didn't. He would always feel like he'd cheapened any chance they had to be together.

Brushing the hair from her face, he palmed her cheek as delicately as he could. His hands were paws with claws or something, disfigured and scarred from cuts and broken fingers and calluses he wore as the badges of his trade. They were like the tats on his upper arms, his back, and the one encircling his ankle made of thorns.

"Sweetheart, are you awake?" he whispered to her ear, then kissed her there.

A smile appeared on her lips and she nodded, with her eyes still closed.

"Abbey, we need to get up. I have to be ready soon, and I want a chance to talk first, remember?"

Her warm blue eyes dazzled him as she shined her bright face like a spotlight into his soul. God, he was going to miss her!

She stared at his lips, covering them with her fingers like she'd done so many times recently. "These lips did so much damage last night, Peter. What you do with your tongue, what you do with your kisses. No wonder they call you a lethal killing machine, my—"

Abbey had stumbled over the word. He knew what it was. It was what he wanted to call her as well. She was his love already. He was certain of it. But it could not be spoken yet. He saw she held back, too.

He drew her up on top of him. She lowered her

mouth to his and gave him a proper good morning kiss, while his fingers traced down her back, over her smooth butt cheeks, and down her thighs to her knees. She shivered under his touch. Her thigh pressed against his hardness.

Fuck it.

He wrapped his arms around her and threw her back against the mattress, clutching her hips and pulling her onto his length. He watched her arch and receive him with that satisfied smile that just drove him wild.

"God, Abbey, what am I doing?"

She kissed his ear and then whispered, "You're fucking me good morning, sweetheart. You're my breakfast and lunch until you can come back here and be my dinner." She giggled before quickly turning serious and groaning. Pulling him deep inside, she spread her knees and clutched his buttocks.

He'd wanted to wake up earlier and take his time with her, if she was willing, but he needed the sleep. Today was going to be an emotional one as they interviewed several ladies who had knowledge of the human smuggling with the Garcia gang. But he needed to come back home to this woman in this bed first. He needed to start the day out right. He needed to rock her world, however short the encounter would be.

As they later peeled themselves from each other,

their sweat merging deliciously between their bodies, he was still out of breath as he pressed her warm body against his and held her as tight as he could.

She gave him a whimsical look. "Peter, I can't breathe!" she whispered, embellishing it with a croak in her voice.

"Sorry! I'm so sorry," he said as he unfurled his arms and gave her space. "I just—"

"No, Peter, it's perfect. I have never felt so—"

There was that hesitation again as she stumbled over that word he'd yet to utter to her. Although he wanted to do so, it was unfair until after they'd talked. She saw his thoughts, he knew she did. In that moment, the understanding of their feelings for each other were both delivered and received. She trusted him fully.

Which was why it was so difficult to get up out of bed. "Come on. Take a shower with me, okay?"

She groaned as he pulled her arm and then hoisted her body over his shoulder and carried her into the shower. She screamed at the cold water on her ass. He let her slide deliciously down his body, their chests together as the now-warm water sluiced between them.

He purposely didn't act on all the little impulses he had as he helped her shampoo her hair, washing all the evidence of last night's love-making off her silky flesh. When she did the same for him he stood perfectly still, his arms dangling at his sides, letting her wash wherever she wanted to and touch any part of him she needed to. In every respect he knew he belonged to her. Peter had never before felt this way about anyone.

She put on a white fluffy robe, wrapping her hair in a towel, while he dried off and dressed. He watched her make coffee and sat down on the couch, going over in his head all the things they had to discuss.

The steaming mug wasn't as hot as her body was under that white robe and as she sat down next to him and presented his coffee, his other hand found its way through the opening to squeeze her left breast.

She set her mug down, pulled the robe off her shoulders, and sat with her full breasts and knotted nipples fully exposed to him.

He whistled, but didn't touch. "Dayum, Abbey. This is no way to have a meeting."

"Oh yes, it is. This will help us keep everything in perspective."

"I like that perspective, Abbey, but you're making it hard to concentrate."

She smirked, angled her head, and pulled her robe back up and over her shoulders, wrapping it across her chest, completely covering up.

"Better?"

He was sorry he'd said anything. But he was running out of time. He set his coffee mug down on the table. "Come here, Abbey."

She was only too glad to climb into his lap. Her finger traced the arch of his ear. He pulled the towel from her head, threw it to the side, then laced his fingers through the back of her head, and pulled her hungry mouth to his. "This is about us, Abbey. This is about keeping this alive," he said as he kissed her, teased her tongue with his, and searched her face. "This isn't about the chemistry we have or the beautiful sex. This is about making sure we have many, many more days and nights like this."

She stopped her toying and rubbed her thumbs over his lips again. "Tell me again."

"This is about us," he repeated as her fingers touched him.

"Yes. I want more of us," her whisper answered him. As she gazed into his eyes, he felt she'd pulled his heart right out of his chest.

He stopped massaging her ass, which was positioned on his thighs, allowing his groin to feel the warmth between her legs. Placing his hands safely on her shoulders, he decided he'd not try to sit down at a table or next to her on the couch. He'd keep her this way, dangerous as it was.

"So here's the thing, Abbey. I can't let anything happen to you. I say this to you not as someone who has—" Now it was his turn to stumble. He decided to just come out with it. "Someone who has formed attachments—" He couldn't find the right words and he balled one hand into a fist. She grabbed that fist from her shoulder and held it to her cheek until he uncoiled it and laid his fingers against her. She kissed his palm, and then pushed it between her thighs.

Now he knew he couldn't do it this way. He withdrew his hand. "I asked you just a few moments ago what I was doing."

She nodded, her eyes dancing, toying with him.

"You answered me correctly. But it's not the whole truth about this attachment between us. This is special, Abbey. This is something I don't want to end."

"Me neither."

"So help me out here. Let me get some things off my chest."

"Okay."

"I've never been married. I've had girlfriends, of course, but no one has affected me like you have. I knew it the first time I saw you."

"Under water. In a wet suit."

"Exactly."

"Your species sort of thing. Biology?" She wrinkled her nose and furrowed her eyebrows.

"*Not* biology."

She gave him a mock frown.

"Well, yes, some biology, of course. But it comes

from here." He placed her palm against his heart. "I mean this with utter sincerity; I couldn't live with myself if anything ever happened to you, Abbey. I'm quick to make decisions, I know, but something about this feels so right."

Her gaze was serious. "I feel the same way, Peter."

"Good. That's a great start."

Her puzzled expression showed up again.

"Being a SEAL, we're gone a lot. We do stuff we can't talk about. Sometimes I come home from deployment and I'm in a rotten mood for a month or two afterwards. I am jittery and a real asshole sometimes. We work it out with each other, other guys on the teams. Some guys don't have that reaction or hide it better. It's hell on the girls—and the families."

"So what are you saying?"

"As good as it feels right now, it might not always be this way, and I want to warn you. I have this radar for bad guys. I feel sometimes like I'm a magnet to them. I see them everywhere. That can be a problem. But it's me, and it's my problem. I get territorial, and I won't let anything interfere with those I—I love."

There, he'd said it.

She put her fingers to her own lips, and her eyes filled with tears.

"I'm sorry. Did I say something wrong?"

"No, sweetheart," she answered through her tears.

"It's all good. Trust me, it's all good."

"I don't want to candy-coat it or lie to you. I'm a piece of work. You hook up with me and you're in for a wild ride, Abbey. I'm not very flexible."

"I think you're flexible. You were flexible last night—" she teased with tears streaming down her cheeks.

"That's a whole different thing. I'm going to be demanding. I'm going to insist on certain things from you. I need to know if you have the strength to tackle all those things. And, believe me, you have no idea how difficult it might get sometimes."

"Why are you giving me all this doom and gloom?"

"Good. I'm glad you see it that way. Like I said, I don't want to sugarcoat it."

"So what is it you are telling me that you don't want to just come right out and say?"

"I want you to go to the police and make a report on Brian. I want you to take precautions in dealing with him. I want you to tell Dante and the other people at the Aquarium that he's not to be anywhere near you. You need to put everyone on notice about you. No more Mr. Niceguy treatment with him. Can you do that, sweetheart?"

"Are you sure?"

"Abbey, I told you some things would be difficult. Even if I'm wrong, this is the safest thing I can insist you do. If I could, honey, I'd take you back to California with me."

Her eyes blinked, wicking away the tears that had formed.

"This is way too soon to be talking about all this, but I wouldn't forgive myself if I didn't ask you to do this. Will you? You can't back down with what I'm asking. There is no easier or gentler way. You have to trust me. Do you?"

"Yes."

He was relieved and exhaled the breath he'd been holding. He placed his hands behind her head and pulled her to him again and just before they kissed, he whispered, "It's because I love you, Abbey. Do this for me, sweetheart."

The long kiss was more than a prelude to sex. He could feel her happiness. He could also sense how nervous she was, and that was a good thing. He was usually one hundred percent accurate about people's character, and what he saw of hers confirmed he'd been right again. And he knew she should be scared. Being with him, committing to him, if they could get there by some miracle, was going to be the most dangerous thing she'd ever done or would ever do.

But, if she let him, he'd protect her until the day he died. Nothing was going to harm her ever again. No one was even going to get close.

CHAPTER 8

S HE KEPT SNEAKING little looks at him as if discovering a chink in the armor or something that indicated he'd not been honest. The truth he'd told her, from his heart, was the most beautiful thing she'd ever heard. The warning he gave her only made her love him more. He made no excuses for being a possessive, fierce lover, the best friend anyone could ever want, and someone she could always count on.

The question in her own mind was whether she had what it took to keep up with him? He'd walk away if she asked him to. He'd stay and shower her world with love. But she had to take that step and do what he'd asked. She had to do it consciously and not by accident or pure chance.

All that remained behind them. From today onward it would be fully intentional. This bond between them was real, after all—love of the highest order. The crazy thing was that she barely knew him. And it didn't matter.

He caught her in one of those looks. "Is there something wrong?"

"No. I'm just wondering what lucky star I was born under."

"My star. You were born under my star. So I could take care of you. It was all predestined. You had no choice in the matter!" He smiled, softening what was a strong comment that made her heart race.

She missed him already as T.J. and Tyler appeared at her door.

"Here you go, lover boy, since I doubt Abbey has anything that would come close to fitting you." T.J. shoved a fresh pair of red, white, and blue boxers at Peter's face. "Go change, but make it quick."

"Now you've given me an idea," said Abbey. "I'd actually like to see what something lacy would look like on him."

Tyler piped up. "Don't try it Abbey. He'd be so pissed."

"I'd be pissed at what?" asked Peter as he returned from the bathroom.

"Here, I'll make sure you have these fresh and cleaned when you get home tonight, Peter."

"That's a serious sign. Already doing laundry for you, sport." T.J. winked at her. She liked the big medic and was glad Peter had such handsome and upstanding men to serve with. They looked her in the eyes without flinching or diverting their gaze. They answered questions directly, even when they were joking with her. They seemed to accept life on life's terms. They didn't preach and didn't seem to judge the fact that Abbey and Peter had formed such a quick, intense bond.

That's probably the way they all do it.

Peter took her in his arms. "You remember what you promised. Don't delay. Get your butt down to the station, and then make sure everyone at both workplaces has the card of the officer you talk to, okay? You make it easy on them, just in case."

"I will. Thank you, Peter."

They kissed and he gave her a light spank on her rear. She waved at T.J. and Tyler and heard T.J. grumble on the way down the stairs, "Shit, Watson, we gotta get you some Red Bull or a gallon of coffee so we can wipe that pussy-whipped look from your face."

Tyler added a big, "Oh Yeah!" to that.

"I'm fine."

"Oh, I got that, but hell if I'm gonna let you shoot a gun or drive a car. I've seen a lot of guys fall, but man, you've got it worse than anybody I've ever seen." He went on making more comments, trying to convince Peter of his opinions, but they'd traveled out of earshot.

She watched them climb into their rented Hummer and waved at him from her balcony. He didn't look back.

Inside, Abbey dressed, gathered her lady pirate outfit for Dante's, packed her makeup and wash kit, and threw in her expensive bottle of perfume she didn't often waste on the clientele at Dante's. But, tonight, she would see Peter again. She wanted every meeting, reintroduction to him to be a showstopper.

She put her hair up in clips, including one she'd brought back from Hawaii that had imitation red flowers attached to the teeth. She was careful not to apply too much makeup so she didn't give the police the wrong impression.

She checked her cell for messages and the time and then clicked it silent, placing it in her purse. She wore navy blue leather tennis shoes with white laces. She checked her jeans and long-sleeved knit top, threw on a red windbreaker, hung her purse over her shoulder, and headed out into the hallway.

The odd scent of alcohol and too much aftershave mixed with body sweat hit her. And not the kind of sweat she'd been enjoying all morning.

Brian's stubble and blotchy red skin highlighted the dangerous wildness of his bloodshot eyes. He looked angry and in so much pain, she nearly felt sorry for him.

Until he pushed her hard by the shoulders and shoved her backward onto her living room floor. He slammed the door behind him.

She moved away from him, doing a reverse crab-like walk while reaching for her purse that contained the pepper spray.

Brian was quick to grab the purse away from her fingers.

The kick to her stomach shocked her. She curled up into a ball, gagging at the pain and trying to get her breath. A sharp pinch and burn at the side of her neck warned her too late of the danger. What had he injected her with? Immediately, her eyes grew lazy but she fought to keep them open.

Peter had been so right about Brian being dangerous, and how she hadn't taken him seriously enough before. She'd been drugged, perhaps was going to die from an overdose of whatever he put into her system. Was he trying to control her or kill her?

But she didn't have time for these unhelpful thoughts. She had to remain strong. As the blackness seeped into her vision, she knew she'd fight him off, if it was the last thing in the world she ever did. Right now, it was the only thing that mattered.

CHAPTER 9

T HE CUTLER HOME for Girls was on a quiet street of well-manicured lawns. Peachtree City was known for licensing golf carts to travel down the main roads, and a series of pathways were created that crisscrossed neighborhoods all throughout the quaint little town. Some claimed there were more golf carts than cars here. It was also said that it had more golf courses per capita than any other city in Georgia. That was saying something when it seemed like the whole state was completely nuts about golf.

Peter didn't much care for the serenity here, and he knew that, as a group, the SEALs would attract way too much attention if they ever wanted to party. It just wasn't his kind of digs.

Tyler was impressed with the sizes of the houses. Row after row of large semi-mansions with picket fences and raised beds of flowers were everywhere, lying under lacy fifty-year-old trees that provided a gentile shade. "My mom would enjoy coming here. She'd love to paint all this color."

T.J. nodded and scanned the lovely gardens as he checked the address he clutched in his fingers. "I'm guessing they hardly need a neighborhood watch program. Use a different kind of toothpaste and you'd get arrested."

Peter chuckled. "That's exactly what I was thinking."

"But the golf would be nice, right, Peter?"

"Amen to that, brother," he answered.

"So how did they get a halfway house for girls here in this town?" Tyler asked.

"Beats me. But man, those girls are probably thinking they've died and gone to Heaven. This has got to be one of the safest places I've ever seen." T.J. shook his head.

He compared numbers to the sheet of paper and announced, "We're here."

They parked against the rounded curb and slowly walked the flowered path to the front door.

A tiny brass plaque was placed discretely above the doorbell, *Cutler House, est. 2010.*

Just as T.J. was about to push the button, they all heard a sound that was completely foreign to the neighborhood. The unmistakable chatter of children's voices and laughter came from the backyard, along with splashing water from a swimming pool.

He rang the bell, and quickly there appeared a white-haired woman dressed in pants and a big work shirt with a brightly colored apron covering.

"Can I help you?" she asked.

"We're the guys from the Navy here to talk to one of your girls about—"

"Oh yes! You're the Navy SEALs. I honestly expected you closer to ten o'clock. You're early."

"Yes, ma'am." T.J. agreed. "We just thought we'd give as much time as possible."

"Very well. Listen, you boys take a seat at the kitchen table, and I'll go get Elaina. Mrs. Foster will get you some cookies and tea or coffee, if you like." She motioned toward the kitchen area, closer to the sounds of the backyard noise. "And, by the way, I'm Mrs. Cutler."

T.J. shook her hand first. Then Tyler and Peter followed suit.

"Thank you, ma'am, for allowing us to come," said Peter.

"Nonsense. Any way we can help out, we're here to do it. As you know, we don't live in a perfect world, gentlemen."

"Roger that, ma'am," mumbled T.J.

They entered a large kitchen with a huge wooden table in the center that must have been able to seat twenty people. Another elderly woman in a flowered apron turned and gave them a warm smile. The kitchen smelled like fresh cookies. Peter had rarely seen anything so perfectly idyllic. It was every little kid's dream of a perfect grandmother's home, reminding him of his elderly relatives in Tennessee.

"I'm Doris Foster. Now you boys sit down here and let me fix you up. You want coffee, tea, water? I also have some sweet tea, our specialty here."

"Sweet tea sounds nice," T.J. said. Both Tyler and Peter agreed.

A large china plate was placed in front of them, and piled high with about twenty warm chocolate chip cookies. "Help yourselves," she said as she placed a small saucer in front of each of them. She returned later with a tray containing three tall glasses of sweet tea, garnished with a sprig of mint.

A very pregnant, dark-haired, Indian-looking young woman in a white smock, entered the kitchen, her head bowed. Mrs. Cutler had her palms on the young girl's shoulders.

"Gentlemen, this is Elaina. Her English is not very strong, but she does indeed have a story to tell." She pulled a chair out next to Peter. "Have a seat, Elaina. These are the men I told you about. No reason to be afraid of them. They're here to help you find your little sister."

Peter glanced between T.J. and Tyler, and he could

see in T.J.'s expression complete surprise.

The girl began to cry silent tears, which she brushed away with the backs of her hands.

"Ah, Elaina. I'm so sorry," cooed Mrs. Cutler. "You want me to get Maria to translate for you?"

"Yes, please, Mrs. Cutler," Elaina said in a weak voice. She chanced a quick peek at Peter and what he saw there melted his heart. "I'm so sorry. My English—" She shrugged, indicating this was perhaps all she could do.

"Thank you for telling us your story," Peter said. "We're here to do anything we can do to help."

Elaina looked blankly between the three men, while Mrs. Foster brought her a glass of ice water.

"I don't think she understands you, Peter," said T.J.

A heavyset girl with long black hair braided like a crown atop her head came bounding into the room. She was older and much more outgoing. She stopped near each of the SEALs, bowing slightly and shaking their hands one-by-one. She took a chair next to Elaina.

After she put her hands on her shoulders, she said, "This is Elaina. She wants to tell you that she was kidnapped at the age of ten and sold to a family in Sinaloa who were looking for a house maid." She said something to Elaina, who responded back in Spanish and nodded. "But she soon became the plaything of the master of the household, and then his sons. She is fifteen now and this is the baby she made with the master or one of his sons."

Peter felt his hands tighten into fists. T.J. had buried his forehead in his hands, elbows on the table.

Elaina spoke to Maria, and again Maria translated. "About two years later, they needed another servant so these men paid for someone to go kidnap Elaina's little sister from her village."

Maria waited for Elaina to say something more. "She says to tell you it was the worst day of her life, seeing her sister being carried—" Maria and Elaina bantered back and forth a bit. "Like she was sleeping?"

"Unconscious?" T.J. asked her.

"Yes, yes, that is the word. Unconscious. But she was not dead, just drugged, sleeping, you know?"

They all knew too well what that meant.

"For nearly two years, she was allowed to stay with her sister in the same room, unless the Master wanted Elaina for sex. He threatened that he would have sex instead with her little sister if Elaina didn't agree, so she did." Maria listened to Elaina say something very emotional and cover her face with her hands. Maria put her arms around her and tried to console her.

The three SEALs didn't know what to do.

Maria continued, still holding the sobbing Elaina. "They took her womanhood. Now she will never have a proper husband. They passed her around between the three of them like she was a pet. I would spit, but Mrs. Cutler has a clean house. These men are devils, and they should all be put to sleep."

Peter couldn't agree more.

"She doesn't have to tell me the rest, because I've heard her story many times. We've met several other girls who come through here, all pregnant, some of them too sick to have the babies. Mrs. Cutler tries to help them find good families to live with or churches to help sponsor them. And she's agreed to help with the childcare when they work. Many of them work here in the golf courses, in the kitchens, the housekeeping staff. Mrs. Cutler is very nice to all of us. No one has to leave if they don't want to."

"Sounds like Mrs. Cutler is a saint," mumbled T.J.

"That she is, son," added Mrs. Foster. "Anyone want a refill?" Maria held up Elaina's empty glass.

Just then, Mrs. Cutler entered the room, holding a fussy toddler. "Doris, can you go change him please while I sit with our guests?"

"Sure." She took the squealing child and disappeared into one of the rooms downstairs.

Mrs. Cutler sat at the head of the table. "Have you told her whole story yet, Maria?"

"Not quite. I haven't told them about Lupe being sold to the man from Baja."

That got all the SEAL's attention.

"Was this a Mr. Garcia? Did you see him or hear of his name being spoken?" T.J. asked.

Elaina nodded meekly, recognizing the name.

Mrs. Cutler interrupted, "That's the name they all come back with. Santiago Garcia. As long as I live, I shall never forget that name," she added. "About the third time I heard it, I called my Congressman and had him over for tea. I attempt to stay under the radar here, trying not to draw too much attention to what we're doing. But this was something I just couldn't take any longer. It sounds like this man is a monster."

"Ma'am. I'm not supposed to tell you this, so you can't say you heard it from us, but we helped put his brother in the ground a few months ago. And this Santiago guy is the one we're after now. God willing, we'll be your spear, Ma'am," said T.J.

"God has nothing to do with it. I put my faith in him daily," said Mrs. Cutler firmly. "But as far as a spear? I put my faith in you Navy SEALs first. I think I can be forgiven for that little indiscretion."

Peter liked the woman immediately, and he could see everyone else did too.

T.J. had been right. She was a saint.

CHAPTER 10

ABBEY WOKE UP in a motel utility suite with a kitchenette and dining table. Zip ties dug into her wrists and ankles. He'd tied a rag across her mouth, which she thought she might be able to dislodge, if she worked at it. She was lying sideways on a bed, secured with a bicycle cable to the metal headboard. She pulled to see how secure it was and found it would cut into her wrists if she pulled too hard. Worse, it made quite a bit of noise, as the headboard banged against the wall.

Her stomach was swollen and bruising, her headache pounded to hard, it made her ears buzz. But as the moments passed, she became more and more alert, gaining in strength. This was heartening.

Throwing her legs over the edge of the bed, seeing if perhaps she could stand, she found she could. But, with her ankles cinched so tightly, her balance was precarious. She sat back on the mattress, extending her legs in front of her, using the headboard to rest against.

Her feet were slightly swollen, because the ties had been pulled in haste and done too tight.

She tried to maneuver her gag by rubbing her mouth against her shoulder, then attempting to hook her thumb under the fabric to pull it up over her nose, but the cotton was too stiff. Spitting into the material, getting the whole area in front of her mouth sopping wet, she nearly had the thing off when she heard a key work the door lock. Seconds later, she came face to face with Brian.

He was carrying packages of groceries. She recognized the recycled plastic tote bags she had from the same grocery store.

"Ah, you're awake. Are you hungry?"

He'd shaved at least, and he appeared to have cleaned up a little from before, but he still had that wild look in his eyes. He was playing some alternate reality game with himself, acting as if she was a willing guest and he was going to entertain her with food and good cheer. In fact, she knew he had something else on his mind.

But as long as he didn't hurt her, she'd bide her time, play along and wait for the right opportunity to do something.

He set the groceries down, and put a six-pack of beer in the refrigerator, along with some eggs, orange juice and other food stuffs wrapped in white paper.

He'd stocked up for a few days, she noted, with the cans of soup and a box of cold cereal with almond milk. He remembered she liked almond milk on her raisin flakes.

"You ready to eat yet?" he repeated his question.

She drew her fists up to her mouth, indicating she couldn't talk.

"Yes, well, we're going to have to use sign language, Abbey. I'm afraid I cannot trust you. Not yet."

She made the mental note he had the confidence he could convince her he wasn't the enemy. There was absolutely no chance of that. That must mean she was close enough for someone to hear her scream.

All of a sudden, nausea washed over her. At first, she thought it was the reaction to whatever he'd put in her veins, but as her stomach lurched and tried to expel its contents, the pain in her belly exacerbated. She remembered the kick he'd delivered, which had knocked her out of breath and landed her sprawling on the floor.

Then panic took over as the bile exploded all around her gag, even driving some up her nose. For a minute, she worried she might suffocate, so she tried to moan and then rocked wildly against the bedframe causing the walls to rattle.

He loomed over her, watching her deal with the disgusting vomit dripping down her neck and chest.

She drilled him a look that told him her opinion of him.

"Abbey, I'm sorry I have to do this. If you'll promise to be good, I can clean you up, but if you pull anything, I'm afraid I'll have to restrain you further. We have so much to discuss. Decisions to make, sweetheart."

He leaned over to brush the hair from her forehead, and she yanked her body away from him, trying to send her legs to the other side of the bed. She rubbed the wet gag around her mouth on her shoulders again to get rid of some of the bile, but at last she gave up. Leaning forward and bowing her head, she cried as privately as she could.

She didn't know if he intended to just scare her, hurt her badly, or kill her. The man in the room with her was as much a stranger as ever. The internal incriminations she felt as she swore at her lack of judgment and her naïve devotion to this man in her past didn't help. She was furious with herself.

But she remembered how Peter had talked to her about staying away from Brian, had talked to her about his wanting the element of surprise. If only she could get to her cell phone or her pepper spray, hopefully both tucked into her purse she saw thrown into a side chair, the contents beginning to spill out.

Brian left and returned with a cool towel and began

to wipe the vomit from her cheeks, her chin, her neck, and then finally down to her upper chest. His other hand lingered on her right breast, and he squeezed, his dazed eyes seeking some kind of erotic response from her which she was quick to not show. She narrowed her eyes and attempted to turn away from him, but he held her shoulder in place while he continued to wipe her face, her forehead, and then dabbed her forearms clean.

Her hair had bunched up into a ratted mess at the back of her neck. She wanted a shower, but didn't dare suggest it. She considered asking to go potty, where she might have some privacy, or better yet, be able to lock herself in the bathroom. She deduced that if there was a kitchen, there would probably be a large sharp knife, which might be the method of self-defense, perhaps something that could untie her wrists.

"Are you comfortable? You warm enough?"

She allowed him to experience the awkwardness of his one-way conversation. If he did ungag her, she'd scream as loud as she could without a moment's hesitation. And that's probably why he wouldn't free her.

"You want a blanket? I've gotten your blouse wet. Maybe I should remove it and you can get warm under the extra blanket? Yes?"

She glared back at him without indicating she

wanted anything.

"Well," he said as he rose and took the towel to the bathroom, to rinse off, "time to make us a little light lunch. I have cream of tomato soup. Your favorite, as I recall."

She wished he hadn't been so observant of her likes and dislikes. She'd burned all memories of him and his tastes from her brain. Now she could see he'd never really let go.

She wondered how he was going to feed her if he wouldn't remove the gag, but she stowed that thought away and averted her eyes down.

Brian angled his head and dried his hands on his pants. "I'll be back in a little bit, sweetheart. And then we can share a nice meal."

Immediately, she began working the gag with her thumbs and finally slipped it down over her chin, resting on her collarbone.

She inhaled and screamed, "Help! Somebody please help me! Help!"

Brian was on her in an instant, his hand covering her mouth as he leered at her, smashing his nose against hers until it hurt. "I don't want to hurt you, Abbey, so don't make me. If I do, it will be *your* fault. We haven't had that talk."

His eyes were red with a ring all around his eyelids. His scent was sickly, mixed with nervous sweat. She'd not noticed the twitch in his left side, or how his lip involuntarily quivered and his left eye squinted. But distressing her most of all was the total lack of concern for her. Instead, he acted like she was the instigator of his problems, that she caused his discomfort and pain. There was no doubt in her mind that he did experience pain. At some point, it would become too much to bear and he'd act out.

He hurriedly yanked the gag up over her nose and mouth, which drove her into a panic that she would not be able to breathe. He ran to the kitchen, brought back a roll of duct tape and cut a wide swath off the roll, quickly affixing it to her mouth and cheeks after removing the gag. But at least her nostrils were not covered.

He pointed the scissors at her mouth, and she stared in horror at him, thinking he was going to stab her there.

"Stop squirming," he whispered tersely. He gripped her chin, puckering her mouth, and angled the scissors at the little seam between her lips. Pressing hard, he snipped. She jumped as the sharp blade caught a tiny piece of her upper lip. Several drops of blood oozed from the hole he'd created in the duct tape. The warm liquid dropped to her chest.

The scissors in his right hand, his left hand contorted her face, hurting her. For a second, she thought perhaps he was going to stab her in the chest or poke out her eye. Terror escaped in a whimper; tears streamed down her cheeks. She shook, knocking the bedframe against the wall, refusing to be quiet.

"Stop it or I'll slit your throat," he said as he held the open blade of the scissors under her chin and let her feel the coolness of the metal resting there. "Don't test me, Abbey."

She knew she was on borrowed time. She was out of options. He pressed the blade against her throat, and she could feel it begin to slice into her flesh. "If you don't stop squirming, I will do it. Don't make me, Abbey."

His wild eyes spoke of his desperation. The tears that filled her eyes were not for herself. They mourned the loss of the wonderful love she shared with Peter, the pain of knowing that they would never be able to be together because of this man. This man had the power to take away her happily ever after. If she could just get the scissors in one hand, she'd find a way to kill him. She might die also in the struggle, but she wanted to end him so he wouldn't prey on anyone else.

He abruptly stood, cursing down at her. Her shaking continued, tears mixing with the blood coming from the shallow wound on her neck and upper lip. She couldn't stop crying.

He threw the scissors into the kitchen and disappeared, returning with another syringe filled with light yellow fluid. She whimpered as he jammed it in her neck and dropped the plunger, his face a mere inch from hers. His sneer loomed as she tried to breathe through the effects of total blackness.

Am I dying? Peter, am I dying? Will you catch him for me and put him away in a cage? Better yet, remove him from the face of the earth. Can you do that for me, Peter? I'm—sorry I couldn't fix you breakfast this morning.

Everything went dark.

CHAPTER 11

THE THREE SEALs exchanged phone numbers with Mrs. Cutler, also giving her the number to the joint task force at Coronado that would lead to their handler, Sr. Chief Petty Officer Collins. Wherever in the world they were sent, the Sr. Chief would know how to reach them.

"You call us if someone else shows up or if you hear anything else about the Garcia gang, okay?" T.J. asked her.

"No problem," said Mrs. Cutler. "I'm going to dance a jig when this cretin is put behind bars or joins his brother in Hell."

Peter was surprised such frank language came from such a sweet older lady. He was fascinated with her warrior spirit.

"Can I ask you why you do this? You could just enjoy your retirement. This is a wonderful town to live in. Why get involved in all this with the girls?"

"Who would do it then? You think the government could do what we do? It's not that they don't want to; they can't. They don't know how."

"But why do you care, aside from simply being a wonderful person?" he pressed.

They had walked to the front door. T.J. and Tyler were already out on the porch when Mrs. Cutler stopped, put her hand on Peter's forearm. "Because I lost a granddaughter a few years ago. She was in Mexico during spring break, traveling with a couple of her girlfriends. They got separated from her chaperone, one of the mothers who went along, and although the authorities found her two friends, shaken up but otherwise unharmed, they never found my granddaughter."

"How long ago was this?" Peter asked. T.J. and Tyler listened quietly.

Mrs. Cutler pointed to the brass plaque above the doorbell. "April of 2010. I vowed that I'd do what I could. We tried for six months, her parents and my husband and myself. They divorced over it. My husband died of a heart attack."

Peter embraced her, not sure if it was the correct thing to do, but he found this wiry older woman's strength impressive. When he released her, he expected to see tears in her eyes, but they were dry. "I'm still here, and I'm not going to rest until we find the people who did this to my granddaughter. I must bring her home, regardless of her condition. She will stay with me here in Peachtree City. If she needs it, she can have the plot next to my husband. But she must come home."

"Mrs. Cutler, do you have a picture of your granddaughter?" asked T.J.

She slipped around the corner and they heard a drawer open. She returned with a school photograph of a petite, attractive brown-eyed girl wearing a cap and gown. "It was her Senior year. She never graduated with the rest of her class. She never wore these in earnest. It's the most recent picture I have of her." She hesitated for a second and then extended her arm, holding it out to T.J. "It's yours."

"Thank you, ma'am."

T.J. and Tyler hugged her as well. Peter gave her one more just before they parted.

Back in the truck, Peter tried to breathe deeply to calm his nerves. He was so angry that such a woman would have to endure so much pain it was clouding his senses.

Tyler and T.J. said nothing. Everyone sat alone with their private thoughts.

"I'd like to call Abbey. Would you guys mind?" Peter asked after some time had passed.

"Knock yourself out," answered T.J.

"God, I miss my kids," Tyler whispered to T.J.

"No kidding. First thing I'm going to do when we get home? Hug them. I always remember after I'm away, always realize I don't do it enough. None of us ever do, right?"

"You're right about that. I can't wait to see them," whispered Tyler.

Peter had dialed Abbey's number but got her voice message, so he left her one. He figured she was cavorting with the shark and angelfish in the big aquarium tank.

"Hey, Abbey. We're all done here in Peachtree. Heading back to Atlanta. It's been an intense few hours. I'll tell you about it when I see you. We should be back in about half an hour, so will see you at Dante's. If there's a change in plans, give me a call. Miss you, babe."

He was struck with how fragile life was and vowed he'd not take anything for granted.

They stopped for an afternoon snack at a barbeque shack near the freeway. The place was packed with locals stopping by to pick up to go orders. The clientele was varied, from men in business suits to mothers with kids. Some college age couples stopped by, and a local amateur baseball team, still in their dirt-smeared uniforms invaded the place and took up the only seating. T.J. directed Tyler and Peter to a picnic bench outside a gas station next door. They devoured the ribs and slaw as if it had been a week since they'd eaten. T.J. did not join Tyler and Peter in sharing a beer but instead crushed ice with his mineral water.

T.J. wiped clean his fingers with the alcohol wipes the kitchen had provided with their order. He carefully brought the picture of the Cutler granddaughter out, laid it on the table, and spoke down to it.

"Well, Miss Chrissy Cutler. You have a mighty fine grandmother. We're gonna see what we can do about bringing you home, sweetheart."

"Amen to that," said Tyler. Peter nodded his agreement.

Peter's phone rang, and he answered without checking where it came from, he was so sure it was Abbey.

"Hey, sweetheart!"

The gruff voice on the other end of the phone was Dante's. "Been a few months since my wife's called me that, but never you mind. This isn't a fun call, Peter."

He sat straighter and watched as T.J. and Tyler perked up, watching him carefully. "It's Dante," he whispered to his teammates, putting his hand over the microphone on his cell.

"What's up, Dante?"

"I got a call from the Aquarium. Abbey didn't show up for work today, and they wanted to know if they'd gotten her schedule mixed up and she was instead at the restaurant. I told them I hadn't seen her all day. You know where she's at Peter? In about a half hour, she's going to be late here too."

Ice water coursed through Peter's veins.

"No fuckin' clue. No one's seen her, then?"

"No, sir. Can you stop by her apartment. Are you close?"

"Yeah. We're about twenty minutes away. We'll go there and give you an update. Has anyone heard from her today at all?

"Nope. She didn't call to say she was sick, or going to be late, or anything. I don't have to tell you I'm worried. This isn't like Abbey at all. Not at all."

Dante signed off and Peter stood. "Come on. Abbey's missing. She hasn't shown up at the Aquarium today for work and Dante hasn't seen her, either. We gotta go by her place and check to see if she's okay."

ABBEY'S CAR WAS missing. Had she had an accident somewhere and was stuck in her car, waiting for help? Peter toyed with several scenarios before he allowed himself the final, most dreaded one. Was her ex involved? Part of him realized it was entirely possible.

They stopped by the manager's office and he said he hadn't seen Abbey all day. He offered to open her apartment door to help check on her, but wouldn't let them have a key. All four of them jogged down the hallway on the second floor until they came to Abbey's apartment door.

At first, nothing appeared out of place. But upon closer inspection, Peter saw a few drops of what smelled like vomit on the rug in the living room. The bed had been made. Everything in the kitchen was clean. But the carpet near the liquid was lined with several ruts in the carpet tufting. The table nearby the easy chair was at an odd angle, and the lamp was not centered on it, like Peter had seen before.

"Someone's fallen here," he said to T.J., pointing out the sharp furrows in the carpeting. "The lamp's been bumped, and the table moved."

The manager stood meekly in the doorway, his hands in his pockets. T.J. spoke to him.

"You sure you didn't see her leave?" he asked.

"No, sir. Let me get back down to my unit, and I'll ask the gardener and the pool man, okay?" He left as soon as T.J. nodded.

Peter called Dante. "Something's wrong. Her car's missing. But it looks like a struggle happened here, like someone fell or knocked a few things out of place."

"I'm on speed dial with the Chief. I served with his pappy, the biggest toughest SEAL I ever met, Mr. Franklin Hicks. You want me to have him get someone out there?"

"I'm thinking, yes. But if she's missing and not in an accident somewhere, I have a good idea who's responsible. You seen anything of her ex, Brian?" Peter asked.

"Nope. As far as I know there hasn't been anyone hanging around lately even before you guys. I'll ask a couple of her friends, though."

"You should call her again, Peter," said T.J., placing his hand on his shoulder.

His fingers shook, but he redialed her number. Once again, he got her voice message.

"Abbey, sweetheart. We're getting a little worried now. Please call me back. We've got the Aquarium people and Dante asking us where you are. Are you okay? Try to get a call back. Love you."

Both T.J. and Tyler's heads whipped up to attention.

Chief Turner Hicks showed up in person. If his father was one of the biggest, toughest badass SEALs in the history of the SEALs, his son was times two. The guy filled the doorway like it was midnight. He brought along two of his deputies and a homicide detective, though there was no evidence of murder. Based on Dante's description of the encounter Peter had with Brian, he could tell their radar was on high alert.

They asked questions, taking pictures of the room, and had all of the SEALs submit their prints to rule out in case they decided to formally treat the apartment as a crime scene.

But when the manager showed up with the landscaper and one of his helpers, Peter's worry doubled.

"He was helping her up, like she was sick, you know?" the workman said. "Her head was rolling around, and I couldn't tell, but it didn't look like she was walking on her own at all. He put her in the passenger seat, strapped her in, and then took off down that way." The helper pointed to the right.

His description matched Brian's. Peter was frustrated because he couldn't look Brian up. He didn't have his last name. Abbey had never told him the name of the winery she was going to be working for, either.

Then Dante called back. "You're not going to believe this, son. One of my girls said she had a LoJack installed on her car before she left California. The police can send a signal and turn it on. If she's not too far away, we might be able to find it."

It only took twenty minutes to hear back from the police scanners that one of their uniforms had run across the signal and had located the car parked at a hotel near the freeway west.

It was only a five-minute drive from her apartment. The Chief asked the SEALs to stand down. They promised they'd not interfere, but would not be prevented from following behind them.

Less than an hour after Peter had gotten the initial call from Dante, Peter, T.J., and Tyler gathered around Abbey's red car in the parking lot at the Suite Sixteen motel and suites.

One of the deputies brought the motel manager with him.

"They're in room 301."

CHAPTER 12

ABBEY AWOKE WITH the bright afternoon light scorching her face. She felt horrible and gagged, but soon realized the duct tape across her mouth could pose a problem. She swallowed heavily and closed her aching eyes. Stirring behind her on the bed alarmed her. Someone's hand snaked across her waist, splayed at her sore stomach, and pulled her upper torso back toward his body, resting spoon-like next to her on the bed.

Brian!

The thought of him holding on to her—not only kidnapping her, but physically touching her—nearly made her retch again. She groaned and tried to worm her body away from his. Her ankles remained tightly secured.

The hand swept her forehead and hair from behind.

"No worries, sweetheart. If you could just find it in

your heart to understand me. All I want is to talk to you. To explain what's going on here."

Abbey knew exactly what was going on. She was the victim, yet Brian wanted understanding and care. The hypocrisy was too rich for her to stomach, and she involuntarily dry-heaved again. Her head was bursting in pain like something inside was going to explode. It wasn't lost on her that the reason for the duct tape was twofold. He wanted to shut her up, and he had no interest in whatever she had to say.

The man had no capacity to care about anyone but himself.

"You hungry yet? You didn't have the soup I prepared for you. Let me go warm it up."

She felt the delicious coolness at her back as his sweaty body left the bed and allowed her a few seconds of peace. She heard some voices outside the window and down below, and for a second, she thought perhaps she heard T.J. or Peter, but she couldn't be sure. The air conditioner suddenly kicked in, the drone wiping out all other sounds. She sighed and closed her eyes again because the bright light stung them. Dehydration likely added to the soreness in her eyes. If she could play her cards right, maybe she could get some liquid. But not too much. She was grateful she didn't have the urge to go potty and all the dangers that that could pose.

Her mind wandered over the events that had led up to this moment. She relived the pain as Brian kicked her, forced her on the ground, and then injected her with some drug, twice. She saw his eyes, heard the rattle in his voice, and smelled his pungent body odor. And then she thought of Peter.

Images of them holding hands, the way he smiled and joked with his buddies over dinner, the talk he gave to the kids at the Aquarium, the whispers they shared in bed as they explored the wonder of their perfect mating flooded back. Her heart filled with sadness until she understood that at least she'd had these memories, and however long Brian would let her live, she'd not give up on those. She'd fight, somehow, to get them all back again.

If only I could get hold of the pepper spray or my cell.

She arched up, her wrists remaining bound, still secured with the bicycle cable attached to the head-board. On her elbow she propped herself up high enough to see the contents of her purse strewn on the seat of the chair in the corner. She saw the red corner of her phone cover, and the black canister that held the spray. If she could get loose somehow, she could execute a repeat defense. She sunk back down to the mattress, feeling weak.

Brian returned behind her and sat on the bed, plac-ing something on the nightstand. "I've brought some nice warm soup so you can have some. Would you like this, Abbey?"

She did want something in her stomach and hoped that meant he'd remove the tape, so she turned her head and looked up at him over her shoulder. Her heart sank.

In his right hand, he held a small white bowl, but out of the top of the bowl was a straw. On the nightstand was a glass of water, also with a straw in it. Her chances of getting the tape removed vanished, triggering another wave of sickness.

She rolled back toward the window, closed her eyes, and forced herself to think positive thoughts. But her spirits were sagging. Unless she could reason with Brian, she had no chance to crack his thick shell of whatever was driving him. She had to continue to hope that somehow she could get through to him. It would be a total mistake to just simply up.

She adjusted her hips, and scooted towards the headboard, attempting to sit up. Brian set the soup down, came over to the other side and helped prop her up, holding her under her armpits. As she sat, still immobile, she noticed Brian glancing around the room. He brought the chair with her purse on it over next to the bed. She stared at how close that purse was and how easy it might be to grab the contents when he returned, brushed everything to the floor, and held the soup on his knees before extending it in her direction. The straw was aiming for her mouth. She saw steam coming from the bowl and, briefly worried that it would be too hot to drink.

Too hot to drink.

Too hot to drink.

His sickly sweet smile nearly ended her composure. He was focused on getting the straw to the opening he'd cut with the scissors, pulling aside a small section of tape and wiping off crusty blood. In slow motion, the hot liquid came closer and closer to her. She leaned forward, as if cooperating with him, her wrists still bound, sore and red, and lying to the right of her thigh. Abbey waited for what she hoped would be the right moment, reveling in the steam, trusting it would be hot enough to throw him off so she could get to her purse.

She inhaled as the straw was inserted into the opening in the tape. Then she pushed up with both fists, aiming at the bowl. The contents flew right into Brian's face.

He screamed and stood up, wiping hot soup from his face. Pulling back her knees, she kicked him in the groin with both feet, sending him sprawling on the floor.

Her feet made contact with the ground, attempting to scoop her purse contents up alongside the length of the bed. She was desperate to reach the pepper spray, but couldn't get it close enough to be able to grab it. Brian saw what she was attempting. He raised his fist to strike her when the door burst open. Two men dressed in black, weapons aimed at Brian's chest, barged in and shouted for him to remain standing in place.

Brian lowered his arm but was admonished to raise both his hands over his head in a command so loud it shook the windows. As the two rescuers barked orders, tears started streaming down Abbey's cheeks.

Brian was tossed to the ground on his belly, his hands yanked behind his back and secured with thick black zip ties. The second man approached, asking, "You okay?"

She nodded, making it obvious she couldn't talk.

"It's gonna hurt for a second. Ready?"

She nodded again. He quickly ripped the tape from her face, and although the searing pain was nearly more than she could handle, she took in a deep breath of freedom for the first time.

Her rescuer grabbed the pillow next to her and wiped away blood flowing from the now-re-opened cut on her lip.

"Did he hurt you anywhere else?"

She held her hands up and shook her head. "No," she tried to shout into the pillow. He pulled it away and continued to use a corner, dabbing her wound. He cut the ties on both her wrists and ankles and she was finally free.

She leaned over, stretching to touch her toes, and then felt the dull ache in her stomach. She inhaled and pulled up her bloody shirt, showing him her belly, which had begun to turn brownish blue. "He kicked me. It hurts here," she said as she pointed to the right side of her rib cage.

"You were lucky, ma'am. Anything else? Did he sexually assault you?"

"No, thank God."

The room shook as she heard pounding like horses hooves. Peter was at the doorway, his face panic-stricken. She thought to herself she must look a fright, her hair all messed out of place, blood covering her shirt. But in a flash, he was at her side. He picked her up despite the objection of the man in black and held her in his lap as he sat on the edge of the bed. He was squeezing her so tight again, she couldn't breathe. She hit his shoulders like she'd done before, pushing herself away from him.

"Peter, I can't breathe!"

His eyes watered, but the relief on his face was like being embraced by everything she loved about home, everything she loved about everything. The best part of it was he was there to protect her, and she knew he would never leave.

CHAPTER 13

PETER ACCOMPANIED ABBEY to the hospital in the ambulance and wouldn't allow the paramedics to exclude him. The tussle was going nowhere when Chief Hicks separated them.

"Would you two school kids quit this? We've got a patient to get to the Emergency Room!" He directed his considerable three hundred pound countenance on the skinny medic who looked barely out of high school. "You tell me what kind of smart is it to go arguing with this Navy SEAL and his lady!"

"But, Chief, the rules—"

"Fuck the rules, son. This man is a lethal killing machine. He can kill you with his little finger. You best remember that next time you choose to get in his way, you hear?"

"Yessir." The medic mumbled and allowed Peter to assist him getting Abbey's gurney into the van. Once inside, Peter turned and thanked him.

"Thanks, man. But you laid it on a little thick, don't you think?" he whispered to the Chief.

"My daddy would have my ass if I did it any other way. Now you stop holding up progress here and get your butt down to Emory. I got a whole pile of paperwork, and I *hate* paperwork, so you best get yourself as far away from me as possible. I'm gonna be chained to the desk for the next several hours, and then I gots an appointment with my wife. You get my drift?"

"Indeed I do, sir. Well, I better let you to it, then."

"Don't go lettin' that little one explore the outside world too much for the next few days. She needs to stay right by your side, you hear?"

"Yessir. I couldn't agree more. Thanks again."

"All right then." He slammed the door shut.

Peter barely had time to slide closer to Abbey before the ambulance lurched, the sirens blared, and they were off for the emergency room. He tried to keep out of the paramedic's way, but he found the tech irritating with how he mumbled his instructions like it was the first time he'd done it. He didn't share the results of her blood pressure, and Peter decided not to bug him further.

Abbey's smile looked like it came straight out of a horror film. Her swollen lip was bright red and caked with blood that clotted up into her nostril. Another dried streak ran down her throat. Since the first chance he had to hold her hand, she clutched his like she was never letting go.

Her tears glistened in full sheets at the sides of her face, and he could see were collecting in her ears. This caused the paramedic to ask her if she was in pain.

"No," she whispered with her puckered lopsided lip as she stared only at Peter.

"So any sharp pains at all anywhere?"

"Just this," she said as she lifted her shirt.

Peter looked at the pink, blue, and brownish bruises that were forming on her stomach and the dark purple bruise that surely indicated a broken rib on her right. Before he could ask, she explained what happened.

"He kicked me."

The attendant gently stroked over her skin with his hand gloved in blue latex, pressing gently and asking for places it might hurt.

"It all hurts, but not like this," she said as she pointed to the rib area.

"Brian wouldn't be in one piece if I'd seen that," Peter said.

"You were right, Peter."

"About what?"

"Element of surprise. He kicked me to knock me over to avoid getting kneed again. I opened the door and he was on me."

"But he didn't—"

"No. He didn't touch me that way."

Peter stood, trying to balance in the rolling vehicle, leaned over, and put his cheek against hers. She kissed his ear. He slid his fingers beneath her head and squeezed her hair, whispering to her, "God, I love you."

She tried to angle her shoulders up to press herself against his chest, whispering, "I thought I lost you. I thought I'd never see you again." She groaned and fell back. The paramedic gently pulled Peter away.

"Not a chance, sweetheart. Never leaving you out of my sight again, if I can help it."

Of course it was ridiculous to say. He'd have to go on deployments. She'd be left behind on plenty of occasions. But it made him feel better to tell her that anyway. She knew what he meant.

The hospital buzzed with activity. It took nearly three hours before all the tests, including a urinalysis could be completed. The sample was turned over to the police as evidence. It was determined the drug he'd used was short-acting and would not be something she'd have much residual effect from, an animal tranquilizer, she was told. The police also mentioned that because she bled it would upgrade Brian's likely charges. And he'd used scissors, considered a weapon. The drugging and kidnapping was the most serious of charges, but there had been evidence of stalking and a host of other things. They were reassured that Brian's chance for bail, due to his apparent mental state, was next to nil.

She was not wrapped for the confirmed broken rib, but given instructions on its care. At last, Peter was able to wheel her out to T.J.'s rental Hummer. All three SEALs lifted her up and placed her carefully in the second seat, strapping her in. Tyler returned the wheelchair. Peter sat next to Abbey, held her hand and kissed her palm as they headed back to her apartment.

"Did they find my purse?" she asked.

"Yup," Tyler held up a blue hospital bag. "Your wallet and cell phone are here, too."

"Oh great. Can I call work?"

"Honey, Dante already knows you won't be in for awhile. I didn't know who to call at the Aquarium."

Abbey made a very brief call to the store manager, assuring her she was not hurt.

"She said the news crews were back. This time they were getting a story we liked. Interviewed half the staff," she said after she hung up.

"You got any ice, Tyler?" Peter asked.

"Sure do." He slapped a white packet he retrieved from the hospital bag and handed it to Peter.

He pressed it gently against her side. Abbey hissed in pain. "Sorry, but it's good for you. Am I pressing too hard?"

"No, it's just cold!"

"Hey, Tyler, got another one?"

"T.J., I think we better get some more of these after we drop them off, what do you think?"

"Good idea," agreed T.J.

Peter held the pack out in front and Abbey turned in his direction, presenting her face. Before he placed the cold pack against her, he gently kissed her. "Welcome back, sweetheart," he whispered.

Tyler and T.J. lead the way and brought her things in while Peter held Abbey across his chest. Once inside, he gently laid her down on the bed, sat next to her and held her hand, kissing her knuckles and palm.

"Look, we're gonna go get a few things you'll need. They give you a prescription to fill?" T.J. asked.

"Yes, but I don't want anything for pain. Thanks, though."

"You want some some soup?"

Her eyes got the size of golf balls.

"Absolutely not!"

T.J. GAVE THEM the news that Kyle had ordered them all to return to San Diego on Monday. Their next deployment had been stepped up. Peter knew that meant they had no time at all, and he couldn't even ask to be relieved of this rotation or be late with the planning and workup.

After discussing their options, Peter made the suggestion to call Mrs. Cutler and see if one of her ladies would be willing to come help Abbey out for a few days. The woman was only too pleased to help out and promised to be there herself on Monday.

"You guys can stay here. No reason to leave," Abbey said to T.J. and Tyler.

"Nah, give you guys time alone. But thanks. We'll pick you up early. If there's anything else you need, Text me," said T.J. "Our plane doesn't come until three, but that gives enough time to get Mrs. Cutler set up."

When the door closed behind them, Peter was finally alone with Abbey.

"They didn't listen. Brought some clam chowder and it smells wonderful. I'll bet you haven't eaten anything all day," Peter said.

She finally agreed.

He balanced two bowls and brought in the small loaf of French bread, placing it on a napkin between them. He was going to feed her the soup, and she took it from him.

"I'm not an invalid," she said rather pointedly.

"Just trying to help out."

"I have other plans for you." Her eyelids were half-closed as she peered over the spoon and sipped the warm soup.

"I'm taking that as a very good sign you'll fully re-cover." Peter's voice had suddenly dropped, husky with need.

"I'm halfway there right now," she responded.

The soup was finished, and Peter removed their dishes. "Shower?"

"Let's talk first." Abbey was insistent.

Peter removed his shoes and climbed up on the bed next to her, propped by the pillows against the wall. He took her hand in his and massaged the length of her fingers, smoothing over every joint of every finger and pressing against certain points in her wrist, the back of her hand, and up the inner side of her forearm. He could feel her becoming pliable and soft, and losing resistance to his touch as her pain subsided.

"That feel better?"

"Divine!"

He picked her hand up and stared down at her palm. "I have to leave tomorrow, but there's no way I'm leaving you behind. I want you to come to San Diego as soon as you can."

"How long before you leave?"

"Maybe a month. Normally, it's a couple of months, but this time, we're in a hurry, and we've been there before."

"You going where?"

"Mexico. Baja."

"Okay. And how long will you be gone?"

"A month, probably less."

He sucked in air. She stroked his cheek with her fingers. "Thank you."

"For what? You owe that to the police, to Dante."

"No, for being you, Peter. For walking into my life and changing everything about it."

He stared into her teary eyes, leaned over and kissed her carefully. Her sour expression when they separated told him her lip still hurt. "So I guess I'll have to use my lips somewhere else, then." He pretended not to notice her sly grin. Coming to his knees, he lifted her shirt over her head, and removed her bra, mindful of her rib. He suckled one of her nipples.

"That feels better already."

"It tastes wonderful. Dessert for me."

Her fingers sifted through the back of his head as he gave attention to her other nipple. Coming up for air, she framed his face with her palms.

"I thought it was all over today. I thought I would never have this again."

"Impossible, Abbey. This was destined from the very first time I saw you in that skin-tight blue and yellow dive suit. I knew it then, and I know it now. You belong to me, Abbey. And I'm completely yours."

Her eyes welled up again. "I'm the happiest girl alive, Peter." She traced his lips with her fingers.

"So San Diego… You're coming with me."

"Yessir."

He liked that she didn't push him further. "But I have one more condition, Abbey. You didn't get to keep your promise to me earlier, but this one is non-negotiable."

He could see she was braced for something.

"Marry me."

"I've known you, what, three days?"

"I think two and a half."

"Is that enough time?"

"You know what I think. I've already asked myself that question, and I've answered it. Marry me, Abbey. I want you to come home to. I don't want you outside our community. I want you safe, with us, close by all my best buds and the wives. If you get to San Diego and you don't like it, well, okay." He was going to continue but she placed her fingers over his mouth again.

"My answer is yes, Peter. Sounds like you don't want a long engagement."

"I'm not really that way. Why string it out and make me suffer?"

She smiled. "Good. Glad that's settled. Now, stop talking and get me naked," she whispered.

Peter helped her to her feet, removing the rest of her clothing, and then walked her to the bathroom. At the mirror, she gasped, getting finally a good glimpse of her face and swollen features, as well as the bruising on her midriff. He watched her accept it, and then turn into the shower.

He was so frantic to get his jeans off him he got his foot stuck. Finally naked, he helped her shampoo her hair, smoothing down the soapy bubbles over her silky skin. He drew her backside to his chest and held her as tight as he dared, kissing the side of her neck. Under the steamy shower he took a position on the tiled bench seat, lifted her by the hips and pulled her against him. She bent her knees at his thighs, moved up and down on the length of his shaft, undulating carefully, presenting her breasts to his mouth.

Without urgency, he made love to her, allowing her to guide him, holding her, kissing her bruised parts, and smoothing over her bumps and ridges, all the dark and exciting places of her body.

She was the perfect compliment to his hardness. She was soft where he was firm. Her moans and passion inflamed him to give her everything he had.

She'd thanked him for coming into her life and making everything different. The real truth was that this golden mermaid had given him the life he'd dared to dream possible.

And for that, he'd protect and cherish her forever.

This is not the end. It is only the beginning. You will be reading more about Peter and Abbey's journey soon.

If you enjoyed this story, won't you consider leaving a review?

It has been a pleasure to write with this talented group of writers in the Magnolias and Moonlight grouping of stories about Atlanta. Here is an excerpt from another wonderful story in this collection by Lisa Kessler.

Magnolia Mystic, Chapter 1:

MAGNOLIA MYSTIC –

Sentinels of Savannah

Book #10 in the Magnolias & Moonshine Series

By – Lisa Kessler

CHAPTER 1

"P IRATES, OR PRIVATEERS as they sometimes called themselves, were actually very democratic. Everyone got a cut and the entire crew elected their Captain and Quartermaster…"

The tour guide's voice faded as Skye Olson made her way toward the stern of the ship. She didn't come onboard to listen to pirate stories. Growing up in Savannah, she'd heard all of them before, even the faint whispers of the pirate spirits that still walked among them. She was grateful every day that she couldn't hear the dead.

She'd have to move away.

But the past few weeks had her thinking along those lines anyway. Catching glimpses of the future was her trade, she'd grown up with the sight, but somehow she'd been blindsided when she discovered Curt had been living a double life.

The deceit, and her lack of foresight, had shaken her to the core. How could she offer guidance to her clients if she couldn't even protect herself?

She stared down at the Savannah River. The water

was always changing, just like the boats that had come and gone from this port for centuries. Was it telling her to cast her sails to the wind and get a new start?

Last year she never would have imagined pondering that question. Indecisiveness used to be foreign to her.

She twisted the ring on her finger until it slid free. The engagement—the entire relationship—had been built on lies. Expensive, costly lies. She gripped the ring tight in her fist. She'd left her shop this morning determined to toss it into the moving water.

But now…

"Tour's up on the bow." A tall shadow fell over her.

She didn't take her eyes off the river. "I know, thanks."

His boots thumped on the deck behind her. "I wasn't givin' directions."

She sighed and glanced over her shoulder. Her gaze traveled up his body, way up, to focus on his dark eyes. "I just need a minute."

He shook his head, crossing his tan muscled arms over his broad chest. "Plenty of minutes are available with the tour. This area's off-limits."

He was just doing his job, but her tolerance for men was at an all-time low at the moment. "I'm not going to touch anything."

His eyes moved to her feet and back to her face.

"Seems you already are."

Heat burned in her cheeks. "What is it with you men thinking you can just make a law and judge us when we question it?" She jammed the ring in the pocket of her jeans. "I'm sick of your shit. So if you want me to move, you'll have to do it yourself."

He raised a brow. "You finished?"

His calm only fueled the tempest inside her. "No, actually, I don't think I am." She matched his posture: chest out, arms crossed. "My family's been in Savannah since it was settled. I know the pirate stories, and I didn't buy a ticket for a tour and 'swearing in' ceremony under the pirate mast. Forgive me for wanting a few minutes peace with the Savannah River."

He pointed to a sign.

Area is for Crew Only

A spark lit in his eyes. "If you'd been sworn in, you might be able to sway me to let you stay."

She blew out a frustrated breath, her hands falling to her sides. "Look, I just wanted to toss my engagement ring into the river without getting arrested for littering. I figured no one would see me from up here."

He relaxed his stance a little. "Must be an idiot to allow a fiery lass like you to get away."

"Please don't get flirty." She rolled her eyes. "I'm not in the mood."

A hint of a smile curved his lips. "Wasn't flirtin', just stating a fact." He glanced over his shoulder. "Speaking of facts, you should pawn the ring. Feedin' gold to the fish won't cure heartache."

"Sage wisdom from a guy working on a pirate ship for tourists."

His jaw tightened, but he didn't take the bait. "Time to rejoin your tour."

She chuckled. "Whatever they're paying you for security, it's not enough."

"It's my boat. My rules."

She lifted her hand to shield her eyes from the sun as she peered up at him. "You own the Sea Dog?"

"Aye."

Skye took a step back toward the railing. He couldn't be much over thirty, if that. And the massive Spanish galleon ship had to be worth…more than she'd ever seen. "Wow. You come from old money?"

He tightened the knot on the bandana covering his head. "Something like that." He tipped his head at the main deck. "Tour's almost over."

"Fine." She narrowed her eyes. "Thanks for nothing."

She stomped across the deck to the tour group, taking satisfaction in the clunking of her boots on the hard wood. Men and their freaking toys. The masts snapped above her head, pristine without a single rip or tear.

Okay, so this was an incredibly well-loved, amazing, historic toy, but still.

She crossed the gangplank after the tour, glancing over her shoulder just in time to catch the hottie pirate climbing up the riggings toward the lookout at the top of the mast. Sweat had his period appropriate shirt glued to him like a second skin.

God bless him, his back and shoulders were so chiseled, Michelangelo would be jealous.

Forcing herself to stop staring, she dropped the ring into the river from the plank. Not nearly as dramatic as she'd envisioned, but the deed was done. She was moving on.

*   *   *

COLD SWEAT SENT a shiver down Colton's back as he lifted the spyglass. She had violet eyes and a fiery heart, just like the sorceress had predicted. Her reading failed to mention it would take two hundred years for the woman to cross his path.

He watched her move down River Street until she vanished into the crowd. He put the spyglass down and leaned his forearms on the railing. He'd given up waiting for her within a few years, and decades later forgot the witch's prophecy altogether.

But the second the trespasser with auburn hair and

violet eyes looked up at him, the old woman's voice echoed through his mind, like she'd been lurking in the shadows as the centuries passed, just waiting.

A woman with violet eyes will signal the beginning and ending of your life.

He wasn't even sure what it meant. He couldn't die, and he while he technically still existed, he wasn't sure it was really living. The only time he experienced the breathless rush of being alive was out on the open sea with the waves pitching the ship. Those moments when Davy Jones breathed on the back of his neck were brief reminders of what his life had been.

Back when dying was still an option.

Colton scrambled over the wall of the crow's nest, ignoring the tourists on the shore cheering and taking videos with their phones. No one climbed riggings anymore. It was a lost art once engines replaced the winds of the gods.

Milestones like that widened the separation between him and the people of this era. A buzz from his pocket surprised him. His grip slipped on the rope. He slid for a couple feet, the ropes burning his hands as he caught himself.

"Fuck," he growled.

Damned cell phones. He'd resisted them for years, but now that he'd opened his ship to tour groups, it was a necessary evil.

He hooked one arm on the rigging and jerked the cell out of his pocket. "Yeah?"

"Colton? It's John."

He frowned. John hated cell phones even more than Colton did. "Something wrong?"

"Eli was driving to Atlanta to meet the Captain about our counter proposal to his hotel plans for Savannah."

"Yeah, I remember." Colton glanced over his shoulder at the gawking tourists and growled. "Can this wait? I'm a few feet above the deck at the moment."

"He was in a car accident."

Colton groaned. "So we'll get him a new car."

"Ye don't understand." His true lineage leaked into his voice. "His injuries aren't healing, Quartermaster."

Colton frowned, glancing at the raw skin on his palm. "What do you mean, not healing?"

"He was air-lifted to the hospital. I'll meet you there."

Colton stuffed the phone in his pocket and monkeyed down the last few feet of the rigging and dropped to the deck. His head was spinning. He stared at his unhealed hands.

Could this damned curse finally be coming to an end?

After checking the anchor line and locking down

the helm, he crossed to the mainland. He needed to talk to the rest of the crew. Now.

The drive was a blur. Colton jogged from the parking lot into the hospital. At the information desk, he struggled to remember Eli's last name.

They changed them every fifty years or so.

"I'm looking for...Eli McShane?"

The woman behind the desk checked her computer and peered up at him with an obviously well-practiced gentle smile. "He's on the fifth floor. Room 523."

"Appreciate it, lass." He was halfway to the elevator before he noticed his slip. For the most part, no one would ever guess he wasn't born in 1985 like it stated on his driver's license, but when he was stressed or angry, his years aboard a pirate ship often colored his speech.

The lights flashed overhead, counting the floors. He glanced down at his hands. They were still raw and they ached.

For years, he'd prayed for this day, but now that it might be staring him in the face...The woman with the violet eyes appeared in his mind. He didn't even know her name.

The doors parted, offering him a respite from his own thoughts. He followed the sign and rounded the corner to 523.

"I'll be damned," he whispered.

Eli was unconscious with wires and tubes running everywhere. Pins poked through the cast on his right leg, and his face was covered in cuts.

John looked up at him. "Worse than cannon fire."

Colton pulled his eyes off the patient to the others. John rested his elbows on his knees, concern lining his dark eyes. He'd been the noblest boatswain Colton had ever sailed with. He was also the one who sent Eli to Atlanta.

"Wasn't your fault, John." Colton shook his head. "Eli always drove those fast cars like a man who couldn't die."

"Might be changin'." Over by the window, One-Eyed Bob held up a bandaged hand. "Cut my finger slicing tomatoes. Nearly bled out waitin' for it to heal."

Bob was the best damned cook on the seven seas, and a fine pirate. Now he owned his own restaurant.

Colton nodded. "Something's not right, that's for damned sure." He glanced at Eli and back to the others. "If Eli never delivered our proposal, you figure the Captain is already in Savannah?"

John straightened up in his chair with a shrug. "Probably. He's a tenacious dog when he sets his eye on a treasure he's got no right to."

"Fuck." Colton shook his head. "He's only got one property left to claim." He ran a hand down his face. "Okay. I'll see if I can find him. What's the word on

Eli's injuries?"

John looked over at Bob, then back to Colton. "They figure he sat in that car overnight with head trauma. Can't tell us if he'll be the same Eli if he wakes."

Colton blew out a breath and approached Eli's bedside. He covered the younger man's hand with his. "You hear me, gunner? It's your Quartermaster. I expect you to get your ass back to the land of the living so you can help us figure this out. If the curse is ending, it's not starting with you. Understand?"

He squeezed Eli's hand and went back to the door. "Call me if he opens his eyes."

"Aye." John nodded, his gaze locked on their fallen friend.

One-Eyed Bob followed him out to the hallway, keeping his voice hushed. "Maybe we need another hit of the cup. We could bring it to young Eli."

Colton froze, his eyes narrowing while his voice was barely a whisper. "You would seriously take another drink from that cursed cup?" He pointed toward Eli's room. "That boy in that bed looks to be three and twenty, but you and I both know he hasn't been *young* in centuries." Colton shook his head. "Until we know his wishes, you keep that grail hidden."

"Aye." His good eye was still bright green, his body perpetually elderly. "Given the choice, I'd like another swallow."

Colton's eyes widened. "Haven't you grown weary of this world? Every day it leaves us further behind."

One-Eyed Bob grinned, exposing a new bridge of straight white teeth. "Aye, but cooking never stagnates. New food, spices, and machines. Why would I allow myself to fade away?"

Colton ran a sore hand down his face. "Don't you ever get lonely, old man?"

He swiped the air. "I got plenty of ladies, Quartermaster."

"Flesh is always plentiful, but what happens when a warm body in your bed is no longer enough?" This conversation was getting him nowhere. "Watch Eli. I'll handle the Captain."

You can follow us along on the Facebook page with links to all the other authors in this set, as well as ordering information for this novella.

facebook.com/MagnoliasandMoonshine

ABOUT THE AUTHOR

 NYT and USA Today best-selling author Sharon Hamilton's award-winning Navy SEAL Brotherhood series have been a fan favorite from the day the first one was released. They've earned her the coveted Amazon author ranking of #1 in Romantic Suspense, Military Romance and Contemporary Romance categories, as well as in Gothic Romance for her Vampires of Tuscany and Guardian Angels. Her characters follow a sometimes rocky road to redemption through passion and true love.

Her Golden Vampires of Tuscany are not like any vamps you've read about before, since they don't go to ground and can walk around in the full light of the sun.

Her Guardian Angels struggle with the human charges they are sent to save, often escaping their vanilla world of Heaven for the brief human one. You won't find any of these beings in any Sunday school class.

She lives in Sonoma County, California with her husband and two Dobermans. A lifelong organic gardener, when she's not writing, she's getting *verra verra* dirty in the mud, or wandering Farmers Markets looking for new Heirloom varieties of vegetables and flowers.

She loves hearing from her fans:
Sharonhamilton2001@gmail.com

Her website is:
www.authorsharonhamilton.com

Find out more about Sharon, her upcoming releases, appearances and news from her newsletter:
www.authorsharonhamilton.com/contact.php#mailing-list

Facebook:
facebook.com/SharonHamiltonAuthor

Twitter:
twitter.com/sharonlhamilton

Pinterest:
pinterest.com/AuthorSharonH

Google Plus:
plus.google.com/u/1/+SharonHamiltonAuthor/posts

BookBub:
bookbub.com/authors/sharon-hamilton

Youtube:
youtube.com/channel/UCDInkxXFpXp_4Vnq08ZxMBQ

Soundcloud:
soundcloud.com/sharon-hamilton-1

Sharon Hamilton's Rockin' Romance Readers:
facebook.com/groups/sealteamromance

Sharon Hamilton's Goodreads Group:
goodreads.com/group/show/199125-sharon-hamilton-readers-group

Visit Sharon's Online Store:
sharon-hamilton-author.myshopify.com

Join Sharon's Review Teams:

eBook Reviews:
reviewcrewsh@gmail.com

Audio Reviews:
reviewcrewaudio@gmail.com

Life *is one fool thing after another.*
Love *is two fool things after each other.*

www.ingramcontent.com/pod-product-compliance
Lightning Source LLC
Chambersburg PA
CBHW060935120626
46557CB00003B/999